FALIK AND HIS HOUSE

FALIK AND HIS HOUSE

A NOVELLA BY
JACOB DINEZON

TRANSLATED FROM THE YIDDISH BY
MINDY LIBERMAN

FOREWORD BY
SCOTT HILTON DAVIS

PUBLISHED BY
JEWISH STORYTELLER PRESS
2021

Cover illustration by
Tadeusza Cieślewskiego Syna

Translated from *Falik in zayn hoyz*
by Yakov Dinezon (Dineson)
Ahisefer Publishing, Warsaw
Copyright 1929 by S. Sreberk, New York, U.S.A.
Steven Spielberg Digital Yiddish Library
Yiddish Book Center

Final chapter from *Der fraynd*
Falik un zayn hoyz
by Y. Dinezohn
June 1, 1904, pp. 2–3
Historical Jewish Press
National Library of Israel and Tel-Aviv University

Published by
Jewish Storyteller Press
Raleigh, North Carolina, U.S.A.
www.jewishstorytellerpress.com
books@jewishstorytellerpress.com

Find out more about Jacob Dinezon at
www.jacobdinezon.com

ISBN 978-0-9975334-2-2
Library of Congress Control Number: 2020951295

געווידמעט מיין אייניקל אַלבערט לעאָ סטיין

Dedicated to my grandson Albert Leo Stein

TABLE OF CONTENTS

FOREWORD

IT'S ASTONISHING TO SEE just how prolific and popular the Jewish author Jacob Dinezon (1851–1919) was in 1904 when *Falik un zayn hoyz* (*Falik and His House*) first appeared in the Yiddish newspaper *Der fraynd* (*The Friend*). In that year alone, Dinezon's byline appeared on articles, several short stories, and two novellas. His works stood side by side with a "who's who" of modern Yiddish literature, including Mendele Mocher Sforim, I. L. Peretz, Sholem Aleichem, Mordecai Spector, S. An-sky, and the poet Simon Frug.

By the turn of the twentieth century, Jacob Dinezon was acknowledged as one of the most successful authors in Yiddish literature. His novel, *The Dark Young Man*, published in 1877, was considered the first bestselling novel in Yiddish, selling copies in the tens of thousands.

Dinezon achieved further acclaim with his emotionally-charged, tear-inducing novels, *A Stumbling Block in the Road* (1889), *Hershele* (1891), and *Yosele* (1899). As Yiddish newspapers began to thrive in the first years of the twentieth century, Dinezon became an active contributor of stories, holiday tales, articles, and longer literary pieces published in serial form.

x / JACOB DINEZON

By the early 1900s, serializing literary works in newspapers was an established technique for expanding readership and providing authors with a reliable income. Authors such as Alexandre Dumas, Charles Dickens, Leo Tolstoy, and Mark Twain contributed serialized novels to newspapers. When Yiddish publications became viable at the turn of the twentieth century, Jewish authors followed suit.

Dinezon's *Falik and His House* first appeared in *Der fraynd* on Sunday, January 17, 1904, and ran in sixteen installments through June 1. Attesting to its popularity, on three occasions, chapters appeared on the newspaper's front page.

The story describes the trials and tribulations of Falik Sherman, a proud and once successful tailor who has fallen on hard times. His house, which he talks to like a brother, is falling down around him and desperately needs a new roof. But Falik doesn't have the money to make the repairs. When he appeals for help from his three sons, who now live in America, they advise him to sell the old homestead and, along with their beloved mother, come join them in their new home.

Falik, however, is not ready to give up all he owns and everything he values. How he finally resolves his dilemma makes for a poignant and often humorous roller coaster ride.

With realistic detail and unexpected twists and turns, Dinezon offers us a heartfelt, nuanced character with all the foibles of an elder, who is firmly rooted in his time and place. There is little nostalgia in this story. Falik struggles with the real-life adversities of a Jew who doesn't want to leave his homeland even though he endlessly suffers in it. This is a perspective we rarely see in English translations of Yiddish literature.

In 1929, as part of a memorial collection of stories and novels honoring the tenth anniversary of Dinezon's death, *Falik and His House* was published in book form. Imagine the surprise that awaited Yiddish translator Mindy Liberman when she discovered these words at the end of Dinezon's novella:

> From the publisher:
>
> This story "Falik and his House" was once published in *Fraynd*. Before his death, Jacob Dinezon heavily revised it, discarded and added whole pages, and had it typeset in book form. He prepared the proofs himself.
>
> The story was typeset until the last page, but he was not able to set the type for the last few lines of the proof sheet.
>
> We present it as it remained at the hand of the author at his death.

The final paragraphs of the story were missing! The publisher knew the work had appeared in *Der fraynd,* but in 1929 there was apparently no way to access the old newspapers to find the final installment. Although incomplete, *Falik and His House* was published as is.

Now, jump ahead to the twenty-first century, the age of computers, the Internet, document scanning, and digital archives. Today, under the auspices of the National Library of Israel and Tel Aviv University, there resides a vast online collection of historical Jewish newspapers and journals. There among the holdings are digitized issues of *Der fraynd.* And there, because of our modern technology, we were able to locate Dinezon's final installment—his final words—for inclusion here in this first-ever English translation of *Falik and His House.*

For those of us who are descendants of immigrants to America, Jacob Dinezon gives us a glimpse into the lives of those who decided to stay in the Old Country. Like Falik, with hope, determination, and hard work, they tried to hold on to their familiar way of life while perhaps knowing in their heart of hearts that the world was changing and not likely to remain the same for much longer.

Scott Hilton Davis

FALIK AND HIS HOUSE

פאליק און זיין הויז

CHAPTER ONE

FALIK HAS LIVED in his own house for many years.

His wife, Matle, delivered and brought up all of their children in this house, and here she experienced all of a mother's worries and joys. When, one by one, the children moved away into the world, Falik and his wife remained here alone again.

His only daughter, Toybele, lived here with her husband after their wedding and gave birth to Falik's only grandson, Itzikl, here. Now she lives in another house on another street.

Falik had bought his house when land and houses were nowhere near as expensive as they are now, and a workingman who could manage to put together a few rubles could still acquire his own piece of property.

And in fact, those were entirely different times and entirely different years in the world.

When Falik was a young man, he was full of energy and life. His short beard was still black and well-trimmed, and his house was still new, fresh, and covered with a beautiful shingle roof.

Falik held a position of importance among the tailors in town, and his house was regarded as the biggest and most attrac-

tive on the street. Now they are both hard up. Falik's beard has
become thick and unkempt, having long since turned white,
and his house has become grimy and old, the shingle roof worn
out in places and completely overgrown with dense moss. Falik
has fallen out of fashion.

He still stands in his place of honor near the eastern wall
in the tailors' prayer house, but now with an old and tattered
prayer shawl on his shoulders. With his neighbors on each side
wearing new prayer shawls with silver collars, he looks like a
lone pauper among wealthy men. And his house, with its moss-
covered roof, has a similar appearance, standing between new
houses with tin roofs and stone foundations.

This has been clear to passers-by for a long time. Now, Falik
and his wife, Matle, recognize it too. Nonetheless, they haven't
lost heart. Matle still thanks and praises God that they don't
have the headache of turning everything upside down each
year to drag themselves into another house like other people
do. "It should never happen to us!"

As far as Falik is concerned, the house is even more precious and dearer than his wife, Matle. He knows, of course,
that it needs work, and doesn't the house cost him money, effort, and worry?

In the good times, when a loose ruble could often be
found rolling around in Falik's pocket, he always invested that
money in the house. Here, the house needed shutters for the
windows. There, the fence needed painting. Today—this. Tomorrow—that.

"There's always something to do around a house!" Falik
would say. Later, when there were no extra rubles to be found

in his pockets, and he could no longer indulge in the pleasure of adding to the house or fixing it up, he still did his best to maintain it. He fussed over the walls, looked after the courtyard, and took care of every scrap that belonged to the house or the yard, just as he tended to the very hairs on his own head.

One could say that in the entire forty years that he has been a homeowner, not a day has passed when he didn't have something to do, or at the very least, something to think or worry about, with regard to the house. It's no wonder that it became a part of his very life, and when the word "I" passed his lips, it always meant, "I and my house."

If Falik lay in bed under his warm quilt, and a fierce wind tore the shingles from the roof, he thought to himself, "The wind is blowing through my bones and tearing pieces of skin from my flesh to be carried off into the cold, wretched world."

If a coachman passed by and accidentally scraped the wall with his axle, Falik screamed after him, "Bandit, how is it that a Jew has no compassion for living creatures?" And like a mother when her child falls and hurts himself, Falik always smoothed out the damage to the wall and truly suffered just as if he felt the pain the house must be feeling from such a brutal scrape.

But not only did he sympathize with his house, but his house, he thought, felt everything that he, its owner, felt. If Falik was cheerful, had occasion to take on a good job, or received a happy little letter from his sons in America, it seemed to him the house literally shone with pleasure. They might even enjoy a little dance together. If, God forbid, the opposite:

troubles, a disappointment, his Matle had a bad day with her rheumatism and groaned, poor thing, or if things became un-settled in his workshop, it seemed to Falik that his house was also discouraged and glum.

Standing in his courtyard early one morning, he noticed how one wall of the house was leaning a little. Falik came closer and sighed. "Old age is no delight, brother! My back often breaks from old age too. Look, cupping sometimes helps me; maybe I should try it on you sometime."

And when cupping no longer helped Falik, he addressed the house again, "A person, a house, both the same. When you get older, you can't stand up straight anymore. I can't blame you for being so crooked. One can laugh at you, but I remember when you were still young, still beautiful, a hero!"

Coming back from synagogue on the first day of Passover, and seeing from afar the house's torn roof overgrown with moss, Falik suddenly remembered that he wore a new hat on his head, the only piece of clothing that he had bought new in honor of the holiday. Feeling a little guilty, he said, "You think I paid cash? In truth, I got it from Hershke the Cap Maker on credit. He asked for fifty kopeks, not to be spoken of on the holiday, of course. And don't you think they would give me a new hat for you too on credit? They would certainly sell me anything on credit, but they would want you as collateral—that, however, they won't get. Give the devil a finger, and you lose your whole hand! Am I not right to stay away from buying on credit?"

Chapter Two

FALIK'S HOUSE HAD five large rooms in addition to a kitchen with a big oven. Until recently, he had no tenants. When his work was still in demand, and he ran his workshop with his own sons, workers, and apprentices, the rooms were all filled. "Children are people," he would say, "and a worker, even an apprentice, is also a person. And a person has to have his place. A person who has no place, doesn't know his place."

When the children moved away, and there was no longer work for others in his workshop, he gave three rooms to his daughter, Toybele, and her husband. Every year, his son-in-law put money into the fireproof safe. He even had the rooms white-washed before every Passover at his own expense without asking his father-in-law to contribute.

Now that his son-in-law had acquired a store with an adjoining apartment and moved away, Falik and Matle were left, just "Grandpa and Grandma." Falik had no choice but to reluctantly let in a few tenants. First of all, so that the house would be more lively, and second, so that there would be something for the fireproof safe and for the assessment which every landlord in town had to pay.

19

For himself, Falik occupied only the big dining room where the old workshop still stood, and the room next to it with the two beds, still pretty and neatly made, just like in the good years.

Not one groschen of his daily expenses came from the rent. If, in some year, ten or fifteen rubles were left over, a tenant's oven, window frame, or something else, which a rent-paying tenant might require from a landlord, was sure to break. And in that case, there wasn't even enough money left over for porridge.

Falik still made his living entirely from needle and thread. A few older householders still kept him on; those who, even if you were to pay them, wouldn't give their garments to anyone else to sew.

If there happened to be a quiet time when Falik sat without a stitch of work, his Matle managed the expenses so cleverly that you could hardly tell that anything was missing on the table. Everything was still as respectable as it should be.

He always had to worry, however, about putting together the few rubles for the fireproof safe.

"With the safe, one doesn't play around!" Falik said. "Before everything else in the world, the house must be insured against fire." And he knew that he wouldn't be able to sleep even one night if the house were, God forbid, not insured. Somehow he always managed to pay into the safe.

Now he slept peacefully, and if another worry remained, it was only that the house became more neglected year by year, and his fussing, watching, and sighing did not help. The roof aged and rotted further, whole hordes of shingles were missing in some places, and when it rained, it began to drip inside.

But putting on a new roof, even of plain boards, would cost nearly a hundred rubles, and where was he going to get it? If not for his worry about the roof, Falik would have considered himself the luckiest man in the whole town, as he always had in the good years.

He derived much pleasure from the children who still lived here, namely, his daughter, son-in-law, and their two small children. From his three sons in America, there was also no trouble. A few times a year, he received a short letter in which they wrote that things were going well, and they were "making a living."

And as a matter of fact, for a few days, Falik had been sitting and writing an answer to their last letter. Falik was never an ignorant illiterate, and penned quite a good letter.

Children,

I thank you very much for your letter that you at least remember to send once every half year! Could a father desire anything more?

I am pleased with your photos, or "pictchas" as you call them—and not pleased. I'm pleased because I see you are proper adults, with your gold watch chains and diamond rings. Are they free in America? Here, even Shaya Miller's son wouldn't indulge in wearing such chains and rings. A sign, thank God, that you are not lacking in bread. However, I am not pleased that in America you can't keep a beard! All three of you, you should remain healthy, have taken off your beards, and that does not please me.

I won't deny that in my young years, I trimmed my beard myself with scissors, but I despise a razor as much as I despise pork.

But I will say what your wise mother says: "Whatever wagon you travel in, you sing its tune." This is probably the style in America, and go behave contrary to what's in style!

I forgive you the beards. God will undoubtedly forgive you, too. But I beg you, along with the beards, don't also convert, God forbid. Your parents are no longer young, and one hopes that sons will one day say Kaddish for their parents. Do you think that would be wrong, God forbid? Or is saying Kaddish for parents also out of style in America?

Furthermore, I am very concerned that Shloymke and Chaimke have given up their trade. Is tailoring already in a bad way in America like it is here? You know, when I speak to local laborers, they say that in America and London, tailoring is like gold, and every worker who can scrape together a few rubles to pay the expenses heads for America or London. Is it true that America is even farther than London?

Again you write that Chaimke serves in the police, and Shloymke works in a "fectra." I've beaten my brains out trying to figure out what you mean by this. What does Chaimke have to do with the police? And what does this mean, "He works in a fectra?"

Of course, you know our neighbor Boruch Moishe the Fool, with his philosophizing, with his witticisms. Do you know what he says? " 'He serves in the police' means he sits in the police station, most likely for more than just not wanting to recite psalms. For me, it's simple. And 'He works in a fectra' means he's working extremely hard." Better he, Boruch Moishe the Fool, should bite off a piece of his tongue. I say he should do some proper work with his evil mouth!

On the other hand, I suspect that what you mean by "serves in the police" is, for example, the same as serving as a soldier here. But what a "fectra" is, I don't begin to understand. I ask you, children, why do you have to speak to us in French? You know, of course, that your father is a simple Jewish tailor, and your mother a simple Jewish woman. So do you have to show off that you are such fine, well-educated French-speaking creatures?

In truth, I wouldn't love you even a hair less if you didn't know a word of French! And I must say to you it's a lot smarter and better mannered when Jewish children speak with Jewish parents entirely in Yiddish, which means in the language of their fathers and mothers.

Next, I ask that when Chaimke's time in the police is up, and when Shloymke ceases working in the fectra, they should take up the needle again.

True, the trade is not a thick piece of bread, but it's always a reliable piece of bread. Of course, one shouldn't be ashamed of one's work.

Children, at your age, I already had a house thanks to this trade. And believe me, at the time, I considered myself to be happier and richer than the whole world. Oh well, now I am out of fashion, and things aren't as easy as they used to be, but it isn't my fault. The world is like this: in the summer, everything blossoms and flourishes. Come winter, everything lies frozen and bare. My summer, children, is over. I've lived my young years. Now I live in my winter, and what would you want? That your father should never get old?

Your own summers are just beginning, children. Don't let the time pass in worthless pursuits. There is no limit to good things and wealth if you work with needle, scissors, and iron. Only may you have no worse a summer than any summer your father has experienced!

And I did not inherit from a rich father or rich uncle. Remember, the needle, and only the needle brought about my light-filled warm summer!

Your mother begs you not to forget that it's time to think about a practical matter. She means arranging a match and getting married.

Children, hear what else I have to say: if you'd like to return home to arrange a match, so much the better. Here everyone knows you and you know all the girls, and also which ones among them are destined for you. But if you don't wish your parents to lead you to the marriage canopy, I ask you for one thing: know with whom you're getting involved and what you are getting into. Children, a wife is life itself. A wise and observant wife like your mother, she should be healthy, is a sweet life! God forbid, a foolish wife, and an improper one, is a life more bitter than death. Remember this, children, and may God protect you from all that is evil, and especially from a bad wife!

Toybele and her husband don't live with us anymore. Either it doesn't suit them, or maybe it really isn't good to have an apartment on one street and the store five streets away. In my house, where they used to live, we now have three tenants. Not well-to-do people, as you can imagine, and I don't hope to get rich from their rent money. I only hope to come out even, which means if I don't lose more paying for damage than what they pay to live with me.

And why should I feel ashamed before my own children? Hear what I ask of you: I lack proper clothing, and your mother lacks the same, so that we can be among respectable people in synagogue without feeling ashamed.

From time to time, we don't have anything to put in our pot, but we laugh about that. However, our house lacks a roof. It's ripped, torn, so that my heart bursts to see its misery. Have pity on your old home, children! More than once you danced around on the roof. Send your father's house a present of a new hat by Sukkos if you can.

Children, until now, the house has been mostly mine, as it is still, but one day it will be your house again. Who knows how much longer I'll live in it? As long as I am alive, don't begrudge me a sound roof. After my death, when my time will come, don't have me leave you an old ruin that doesn't even have a roof.

Toybele and her husband will tell you how clever Itzikl is. You can believe them. Indeed, Itzikl is a fine, thriving boy, he should live to be a hundred and twenty. But the girl, Itinke, is a sickly child. Your mother says that Itinke, poor thing, has some sort of rickets in her side, but the doctor says that it's an English ailment. From where would such a child get an English ailment? Let evil befall me if I know! Her grandfather probably hasn't touched English merchandise in twenty years.

Anyhow, who would dare contradict a doctor with a degree? Just now they are applying his remedies: bathing, good food, fresh air. Will it help? I don't know, but it can't hurt.

What else can I write you? We are all, thank God, healthy. The town stands in the same place as always. The small house across the way is completely empty now. Sometimes after dark, it's dangerous to go out because all kinds of thieves spend the night in the empty house. Fools say that demons have gathered in the house. I don't believe in that nonsense. But some people claim that Shaya Miller has bought the place and will replace it with a big, three-story apartment building by this summer. The street will, because of this, have a completely different appearance.

Reb Yisroel, the old synagogue cantor, has died. An old man of eighty-five years, may we live as long!

Be well, don't forget the house for your father's sake, and don't forget your father—for the sake of his house.

I write this because sometimes there's a danger that if you ask children for help with something, they may become angry, and stop writing altogether. But I tell you, whether you send a roof or not, to your parents you are good, beloved, and dear children, and you should not be angry with us.

And again, be well.

> From me, your father, Falik Sherman,
> and from me, your mother, Matle Sherman

CHAPTER THREE

As DIFFICULT AS it was for Falik to write the letter to his children, it was even harder to send it off. He was dependent on his son-in-law's goodwill to address it, and his son-in-law refused to help unless Falik crossed out the few lines requesting money for a new roof.

"Tell me frankly, why don't you want me to ask?" Falik inquired.

"Because it doesn't seem right that you should ask people who have absolutely no interest in your house, before you ask me, someone who is quite interested," his son-in-law explained.

"So much the better," said Falik, prepared to rewrite the whole letter. "I beg you, if you take a real interest in the house, as you should, I'll leave them in peace."

"Believe me, Father-in-Law," said the son-in-law, "it does interest me, but I must tell you that the entire house is not worth the cost of a new roof."

"But if we cover it with a new roof, it will be worth something again!" Falik replied.

"Do you know, Father-in-Law, how your house will look with a new roof?"

"How?"

"Like a young head on old shoulders!" said the son-in-law, smiling at his own witticism.

"Who cares how it looks!" said Falik angrily. "Without a new roof, it will be difficult to continue living in it. And I must live in my house! Jokes won't get me a roof. Either lend me money for a roof or, if not, let me mail the letter."

"Do you know what I've been thinking?" said the son-in-law. "It would be better for both of us if you would just sell the house, take the few rubles, and move in with me. We can all live together the way we did before."

"No, my son. You know what's better for you, and I know what's better for me! And it seems to me that in old age, it's just not right for me to live with my children as long as there is no real need for such nonsense."

Insulted, his son-in-law asked, "Why not, Father-in-Law? Have I ever, God forbid, offended you? Are you not a welcome guest when you come over to bless Itzikl's tzitzit or read the bedtime prayers with him?"

"I can't complain about you, my son," replied Falik. "Truthfully, you have never shown any disrespect. But do you know what I'm afraid of?"

"What?"

"I'm afraid that things are the way they are now only as long as I have my own home. If I want to come over, I come over, and if I don't—I don't. It will be completely different, my child, when I no longer have my own place, and must stay with you. Children living with parents never cause resentment, but parents staying with their children become burdens, especially when they are dependent on their kindness."

"But you will have a few rubles of your own, Father-in-Law, and you will always have a choice," insisted his son-in-law. "If you're happy living in my house, you'll live in my house. If you find it unpleasant, you'll rent an apartment somewhere else. I'm not tying you down with a contract!"

"But tell me," Falik answered, "why does it pay for me to give this a try? What will you get out of it?"

"It's worth your while," replied his son-in-law, "because this way, you'll be done with worrying about putting a roof on your old ruin. And it's worth it to me because if you and my mother-in-law live with us, Toybele will be able to help me in the store. Now, she's tied to the children from early morning until night, and the store is wearing me out. You can't imagine, Father-in-Law, how hard it is that I don't have anyone I can trust at the store to keep an eye on the customers or the clerks if need be!"

Falik thought for a moment, and the son-in-law began to think that his words had made an impression on his father-in-law. After a few minutes, Falik turned and said, "But all this, my son, has nothing to do with the address. It seems that you are holding the address hostage, which indicates that you don't trust me. Why then do you expect me to trust you?"

His son-in-law had no answer and soon wrote down the address.

But it didn't end there. The next day, Falik's daughter, Toybele, came crying to her mother, complaining how hard it was to manage without her. She hoped her mother would help talk her father into selling the house so that they could all live together. It would be better for their shop, for her small children, and indeed, for her mother and father as well.

Matle thought that it stood to reason that Toybele was probably right, even though she didn't consider living with children to be any great pleasure. But on the other hand, what wouldn't a mother do for a child?

And really, what did she have to fear? If her children appreciated the sacrifices they were making by giving up their own house, then she as a parent could certainly accept the situation, even if living with children wasn't as good as being the mistress of her own home. But if her children forgot that their parents were doing them a favor, and convinced themselves they were only there for handouts, she could always say, "Dear children, don't do us any favors. Live happy and content. You'll see, we can make it in our own world without depending on your generosity."

When Matle made her reasoning clear to Falik, he replied, "I would never have believed that the saying 'long on hair, short on common sense' applies to my Matle as it does for other women. Now I see that there is not even one truly wise woman in this world. Foolish Matle, how can you not understand that our faithful son-in-law is interested not in the Haggadah, but in the matzah ball soup? He doesn't want me, and he doesn't want you, not even as an unpaid maid in his house. His concern is for the few rubles the house will fetch if I sell it. Do you understand what this is about?"

"What proof do you have?" asked Matle.

"You want proof? Here is an indication. I'll say to him, 'My son, as long as you have your heart set on having Toybele help you in the store, why do you need me to sell the house? Move back in with us. Your mother-in-law and I will be able to help you with the children, they should be well, and Toy-bele will be able to help you in the store.' You'll see, Matle, how he'll squirm!"

"But it's too far from the store," Matle said, ready to provide an excuse for her son-in-law.

"'Too far' is a pretext, Matle! My enemies should have to live in this world the way he had to move clear out of our house and take on the expense of his own apartment."

And Falik applied the test. He told his son-in-law that he had no advice for him other than to move back in with him so that Toybele would not be tied down with the children. His son-in-law hemmed and hawed and twisted his words until it was like olive oil rising to the top of water. He finally admitted that he was really only interested in the few rubles that his father-in-law would get for the house. For the sake of the few rubles, he wanted his in-laws to live with him.

And when his son-in-law was done disgracing himself, he twisted the knife a little further, reminding his father-in-law that he, the son-in-law, was a respectable proprietor and his father-in-law just a tailor. Were he to own even seven houses, he would still remain a lowly tailor and never a property owner of any standing.

Returning home, Falik said to his house, "Listen, brother, there is a saying in the world, 'Sons-in-law are demons,' and so it is! I envy you that you are a house, and you have no daughter and no son-in-law on her account!"

Chapter Four

As Falik mentioned in the letter to his children, the little house opposite Falik's window that Shaya Miller had bought made Falik's life miserable.

The house once belonged to a wealthy landowner who had long since died and left the little orphaned house to his heirs. After his death, a pair of tenants lived there, who, without a landlord to pay attention, turned the place into a complete ruin. For two years, it stood empty and forlorn. Window frames were ripped out, holes that were once windows were boarded up, and the fence was broken.

Anyone and everyone pulled off whatever he could from the house, and the town's goats were kept there during the day when they could not join the flocks in the field. At night, it became a haven for drunks and thieves who had no other home.

Everyone said that demons and ghosts had moved in, and people were afraid to walk past it after dark. But this isn't what bothered Falik. The little house brought on sad thoughts. In it, he saw an example, a moral lesson, about his own house, God forbid. And it often occurred to him that all those new houses

on the street, the insolent young folk on their stone foundations, looked and gestured at their poor neglected neighbor
with pride and arrogance, in the same way young people look
at a forlorn pauper who no longer has the strength to stand on
his own two feet.

But his own house, it seemed to Falik, looked with compassion on the sick, orphaned neighbor across the way. Just as
he, Falik, still remembered how the sun once shone so beauti-
fully in the now ripped out windows, so his house was bound
to also remember. Those new houses were young scoundrels,
but it was their world these days!

"Wait, brothers," he sometimes imagined saying to them.
"There may come a time when you are no richer or younger-
looking than this little house. Better to be smart, you young
people, and learn a lesson from it, from this very ruin!"

And Falik waited impatiently for Shaya Miller to finally
give the lonely old place its due, and undertake to build a
house, a palace, which would be a feast for the eyes.

Although Falik had not constructed his own house—he
had bought it already completed—he nonetheless considered
himself an expert on houses. In any case, if you have owned
your own house for almost forty years, he told himself, you
become an expert on houses!

And he had always had a soft spot for a fine building. He
sometimes allowed himself a few minutes of pleasure as he
stood in front of a beautiful building that caught his eye. If
Fat Shaya would only ask me, Falik thought, I would show
him how to build a house that would be quite a jewel for the
whole street!

The lot was big enough, and Shaya, who possessed the legendary wealth of Korach, had the money to build. He could certainly construct something beautiful and substantial here.

But Shaya took his time. He neither consulted Falik nor undertook to begin construction himself.

"If I had a tenth of Shaya's money," Falik once said to Matle, "do you think I'd build a house across the way?"

"What would you do then?" she asked.

"First, I would refurbish our house, lay a good foundation, straighten everything, put in new windows, and cover it with a tin roof. Then our house would laugh at and outlive all the other houses in the neighborhood. On the lot across the street, I'd plant handsome trees in the front and make a little garden with pretty flowers, a delight to look upon! In back, you'd see, I'd build Pithom and Ramses."

"Dreams!" replied Matle. "I would, I could! You're better off doing your work, so your head won't ache on account of Shaya!"

But early one morning, around Shavuos, Falik saw through his window that workers had crawled up on the roof of the wreck across the way and were starting to demolish it.

"Matle," Falik shouted happily, "live long enough and you see it all! They're finally tearing the roof off that old house!"

"So why are you in such high spirits?" asked Matle.

"You're a woman. What do you know about these things?"

"Go sit and sew," Matle scolded him. "It's just before the holiday, and you're swamped with work!"

And Falik regretted that Shaya had chosen to start building right before the holiday, just when he had no time to watch.

Although it was hard for him to sit inside in his workshop, he needed to finish the work. A Jew has new clothes made only for the holidays. But as Falik sewed, his heart was outside in the street where they were tearing down the house.

Just before dark, right before a workingman would light his lamp, Falik threw on his coat and went outside to see how things stood. The house had been completely demolished, and its bones—the boards and old wooden planks—thrown into a pile.

Children dug among the rotted boards and collected the yellow powder, useful for nursing mothers. Other little rascals yanked out rusty nails, easily pulling them out with their thin fingers.

"What do children know?" Falik said to himself. "Of what use are old nails to them? But for children, this is an activity too, so they don't stand idle!"

Falik looked over the old boards and speculated, "If Shaya would just let me have a bit of wood for a few rubles, I would be halfway to repairing my roof. From such a mountain of timber, why shouldn't I pick out a few decent planks to fix my roof? Even the beams could come in handy to prop up my fence. After all, what have I got to lose if I ask? Why should I be afraid of him?"

And at that very moment, Falik chanced to catch sight of Shaya.

"Good afternoon, Reb Shaya! Evidently, you are destined to have me as a close neighbor."

Shaya smiled pleasantly, as if very pleased to have Falik next door.

"Why are you looking over the old wood, Reb Falik?" he asked.

"Sell it to me, Reb Shaya," Falik requested, almost begging.

"Why do you need the wood?"

"Do I know? Whatever you let me take, I'll use for my house," answered Falik. "Some to fix my roof, some to shore up my fence. Do you need to ask why a homeowner would want a little wood?"

"But listen, Reb Falik," Shaya responded in a friendly manner. "Will you believe what I'm going to tell you?"

"Why not?"

"So listen to what I have to say. It seems to me that it would be a pity to spend even one groschen on your house."

"For me, it's an even greater pity," answered Falik, "that from year to year, my house deteriorates further. Do you think I don't know that my house needs a major operation? I only wish I had the two hundred rubles I need to make it hold its own among respectable houses once more!"

"You are making a mistake, Reb Falik. You can't sit a young head on old sagging shoulders and a broken body! Don't talk yourself into it! And I tell you that every ruble you spend on your house is like throwing it into the mud."

Falik glared at Shaya.

"You resent that I'm telling you the truth?" asked Shaya. "Your house is old, sick, and crooked. There's the whole truth for you, Reb Falik."

"And what am I?" answered Falik. "Not old, not sick, not crooked? Reb Shaya, we—I and the house, I mean—were once

young together. Together we both grew old. I want to continue to maintain body and soul. Why shouldn't I want the
house to live on as well?"

"And if you would listen to me," replied Shaya, "I would
advise you to sell the house and the lot to me. Take the few
rubles, deposit them in safe hands for a small percentage, and
have something to put towards rent. Be done with worrying
about a roof that leaks, walls that slant, and a fence that drags
on the ground."

"Reb Shaya," said Falik sharply. "I'd like to buy the little
bit of wood from you. If you're interested, sell it to me. What I
do with my house is my business. And I'm not senile yet. I know
what's good for me and what isn't."

"How about this, Reb Falik?" said Shaya. "I have a different proposal for you. We'll discuss your house another time.
Maybe you'll be smarter and more reasonable then. In the
meantime, you say you want to buy the old wood from me?
Good! I'll let you have the wood, and not even for cash. Take
the wood and let me store my bricks in your courtyard until
the house is ready."

Had he been in better spirits, Falik would have been happy
with the trade. His courtyard was big enough, and what harm
would Shaya's bricks do? But at that moment, Falik was so irritated that Shaya had the nerve to say, "Sell me your house,"
that he thought the request to store the bricks was just an excuse. What Shaya really wanted was Falik's courtyard and
house. He'd best not give him a foot in the door.

"Thank you for your generosity!" Falik replied. "I need my
house for myself and my tenants. I don't need your lumber. It

was just nonsense, thinking for a minute that it would be useful for something. Good evening!"

"In my whole life," cried Shaya, "I've never seen such arrogance from a poor man!" But before Shaya could say more, Falik tore himself away and didn't look back.

"Reb Falik," Shaya shouted after him, "listen to what I'm telling you. A poor man, even if he does own a bit of property, has no business acting so high and mighty!"

"Reb Shaya," Falik answered in return, "Listen to me. A wealthy man has no right to devour the whole world!"

And with these words, Falik went back into his house to say his evening prayers, swallow a bit of supper, and return to work. It was almost the holiday. Time was short and valuable.

CHAPTER FIVE

ONCE HOME, FALIK washed his hands and began to say evening prayers. But Shaya stood in the way. Instead of praying, Falik felt as if he were quarreling with Shaya. Shaya said to him, "You'll become smarter and better yet!" And Falik answered, "I don't want to become smarter, and I don't want to become better!"

"Live long enough, and we'll see," said Shaya, and Falik answered, "Not on your life!"

When he spit during the Aleinu prayer, he thought, "I spit on you, Reb Shaya. You make me laugh. If I don't want, I don't want. Try and make me!"

He found no pleasure in supper. He tasted a few spoonfuls and soon pushed the plate away.

"Why aren't you eating?" Matle asked.

"It's altogether tasteless!" answered Falik. "Maybe it needs a little salt or something?"

"You don't have an appetite and that's all there is to it!" Matle observed. "I'll leave it to warm for later. You'll be famished by bedtime. You'll probably stay up late tonight?"

Without answering, Falik took up his work again.

He hoped that sewing would chase away his bitter thoughts, but the thread kept tangling. Waxing it didn't help, and the needle strayed from its path more than a few times.

"What does this have to do with you?" Falik asked the needle. "Just be faithful to me. Never mind Shaya or his grandmother either! You see, God forbid, if I'm not able to tell you what to do, perish the thought, things will be miserable indeed."

It seemed like the needle understood her master and promised to be loyal. Falik buried himself in the sewing and forgot all about Shaya.

"Maybe you'll eat now?" Matle inquired a few hours later before going to bed.

"Let me have it," answered Falik. "As a matter of fact, I'm dying of hunger." When he sat down at the table, he ate with a hearty appetite.

Wondering why the same supper was so tempting now, Falik remarked to Matle, "Before, it had no flavor, and now it's fit for a king!"

"When the mouse is stuffed, flour is bitter!" replied Matle.

"Stuffed, you say? Do you think I've put anything in my mouth since lunch?"

"Why else couldn't you eat earlier?"

"My stomach wasn't quite right," answered Falik. "That short, fat fellow disturbed my digestion."

"Who?" asked Matle.

"Shaya Miller, that's who! Loaded with money just like Korach, and he wants to swallow up the whole world in his huge stomach."

"What does he have to do with you?" asked Matle. "What kind of business could you have with Shaya Miller?"

"I tell you, the man is never satisfied!" replied Falik. "He has his eye on our house. But let's not talk about it now before going to bed. We don't want to dream about it."

When Falik finished his supper, he said, "You know what I think, Matle? Go ahead and prepare the beds. I'm so tired and sleepy, it's as if I've been awake for ten nights. I think I'm better off waking up early to sew while you are still asleep."

Right away, Matle made up the beds. Falik finished reciting the blessing after meals, undressed, and began to say the bedtime prayers, but fell asleep before he was done.

And his hunch turned out to be right. Shaya Miller came to him in a dream.

And indeed, Falik dreamt that as he sat sewing in his workshop, the thread snagged. He struggled to untangle it, and when it was finally free, he no sooner gave a tug on the needle than it stopped again. A knot in the thread! Ripping out the thread, he continued sewing, but this time when he gave the needle a yank, the whole seam came apart. Suddenly, the door opened and in came Shaya Miller with his plump stomach and his face oddly cheerful, dripping with animal fat.

"Good evening, Reb Falik!" Shaya said in the dream. "I've come to have you measure me for a coat and two pairs of trousers for Shavuos."

"But there's only one week before the holiday, and when will I have time to do it?" asked Falik.

"You have it wrong," said Shaya. "It's still two weeks away! Here is a calendar, take a look. You'll see that I'm right."

And Falik checked the calendar in his dream, and so it was, two full weeks remained.

"Why did I think there was only one week left?" he asked.

"That's what you thought in your dream. In reality, there are two weeks, so you'll have plenty of time to sew me a coat and trousers," Shaya answered in the dream and started to button up so he could be measured.

And it looked to Falik as if Shaya's coat wouldn't close.

"Some incompetent tailor must have made your suit!" said Falik. "I'll sew a coat for you. It will actually be only a little wider, but the coattails will overlap by half a yard."

"Don't flatter yourself, Reb Falik!" answered Shaya. "A poor tailor has no business being arrogant! It's not at all the fault of the other tailor. It's just that my stomach has grown a bit."

And it seemed to Falik that he was dissatisfied with Shaya's reply for some reason, and answered, "If that other tailor, who sewed your coat, pleases you—even though the coat is too tight and too short—then be my guest, go see him! I will not sell you my house."

He had no idea why he mentioned his house.

"I don't want to buy your house, Reb Falik," said Shaya. "Live in your house in good health."

"The silliest thing in the world would be to sell your house to Shaya Miller."

"And who are you?" wondered Falik. He was sure he had been speaking to Shaya just a moment earlier.

"You don't recognize me, Father-in-Law? Obviously I'm your son-in-law, your Toybele's husband, your grandson Itzikl's father." Now it was his son-in-law who was speaking.

"But your stomach, good heavens, your stomach!" shouted Falik. "You have Shaya's stomach. How did you come to have Shaya's stomach?"

"That's just the way it is," said his son-in-law. "Just measure it quickly, because my stomach keeps growing."

And Falik picked up his measuring tape, but Shaya's stomach kept expanding as if filled with yeast. The tape was too short to measure it.

All at once, it seemed to Falik that Shaya was standing at his gate and instructing the workers to carry carts of bricks into the courtyard. Falik jumped out of his house to stop them, but a whole gang of boys surrounded him and flung yellow wood powder and rusty nails at his face. The workers wheeled the carts of bricks into the yard.

"Sold is sold!" shouted Shaya. "Your son-in-law is a witness that I have bought your house! Look, it's in black and white."

And Falik noticed a sheet of paper in Shaya's hand and thought he remembered that it was true, he really had sold him the house. He couldn't recall how it happened, but his heart ached with regret. "Take back your money, I don't want it. I can't. I mustn't sell you my house!" he cried out. But Shaya just laughed.

"You may as well talk to the wall!" replied Shaya. "Your screaming and crying will be as helpful as cupping a corpse. A purchase is a purchase!"

"Thief! Murderer! What do you have against me?" Falik pleaded in his dream. "You came to be measured, and in the meantime, you have stolen my house, my life!"

Shaya picked himself up and left. Falik ran after him, but Shaya walked quickly, almost flying through the air. Falik's feet felt like lead. He could barely manage to take a step. His chest hurt, and he wanted to scream, but he'd lost his voice. Suddenly, he realized that he was standing near Shaya's mill. Sacks of flour lay everywhere. Shaya said, "Maybe you think these are sacks of flour? Take a good look, and you'll see that the sacks are filled with gold, and I am giving all of this gold to you for your house."

"Father-in-Law, take the gold and let Shaya choke on the old ruin with no roof." There stood Falik's son-in-law, beckoning to him, but Falik was afraid to look and wanted nothing to do with him.

"Falik, come home," he thought he heard Matle shout.

"Our house—it's still standing?" he inquired. "Shaya hasn't knocked it down yet?"

"Fool," she said to him in the dream. "This is all just a dream! You didn't sell, and Shaya didn't buy. Come home, don't look at Shaya's gold. It's not gold, it's just a dream!"

And it appeared to Falik that he went over to Shaya, spit in his face and said: "I spit on you! I'm as rich as you are. Your gold is a dream, and my house is for real. Matle, come on. Let's go home."

And he thought he headed home with Matle, but they lost their way. The streets were not the same as before, and he didn't understand why he couldn't reach his house. Just then, he encountered the postman who handed him a letter. Matle opened the envelope and found a draft for one hundred rubles. The children had sent money for a new roof.

"Listen, Matle," he said to his wife, still dreaming. "It pays to have children! The trouble we go through until we turn them into adults is worth it. In our old age, they give us joy, even though they're far off, all the way in America. What would we have done now without a roof? Come, I want to go to the lumber yard and see the workmen."

"Your happiness is in vain, Husband," answered Matle. "Our house has already been sold! Shaya has just knocked it down, and we don't even have a place to lay our old heads."

"What are you saying, Matle?" It seemed he was shouting, but he almost couldn't hear his own voice. "You said this is all just a dream!"

"I tricked you," she answered. "Sold is sold. It's hopeless. Husband, we no longer have a house or a home. I will go to Toybele's, and you will stay in Shaya's mill."

"No, no, Matle, I don't believe you. It's a dream. A dream, I tell you. In reality, this can't possibly happen," Falik consoled himself in the dream.

"Here, see whether this is a dream or the truth," said Matle.

And Falik saw that not even the slightest trace of his house remained. The whole yard was filled with Shaya's bricks. Off to the side, the limbs of his house lay scattered about. He recognized every piece of wood and where it had come from in the house. Every board looked at him mournfully, as if with a thousand eyes bathed in tears.

He thought he heard grumbling from the old shingles, torn off from the roof. "What did you have against us? We could have lived another hundred years. And we were still alive when you sold us."

In the middle of the street, Falik seemed to spot his two beds, made up with the woolen quilts and cushions in their white pillowcases. Close by stood his workshop with scissors and pressing iron, but the clothing he was working on wasn't there.

"Where is the cloth? It doesn't belong to me. They'll throw me in prison," cried Falik. He burst into such loud tears in his sleep that Matle actually heard his wild sobbing, leaped out of her bed in terror, and began to tug and shake her husband to awaken him from his heavy sleep.

Falik awoke frightened and wrung out. It was as if the dream still held him in its powerful hands, squeezing his chest.

"What did you dream that made you howl and sob so?"

"Again you talk about dreams? Do you want to trick me again?" answered Falik, uncertain if he was talking in his sleep or actually speaking.

"Falik, what are you saying? What's the matter with you? I haven't even had a chance to say the blessing for washing hands yet. And when have I ever tricked you? Pull yourself together."

"Where am I?" he asked, still not sure if he was really awake.

"Where should you be? You're in your bed."

He tapped the bed, the pillows under his head, and the wall next to the bed, but even that wasn't enough to convince him that he was no longer dreaming and was now really awake and talking to his Matle.

"Open a shutter," he pleaded. "Let me see what's going on here with my own eyes."

Matle quickly opened a shutter. A stream of gray early morning light broke into the bedchamber. Only then did Falik begin to believe that it had all been a dream, and now he was truly awake.

"Matle, let me have the pitcher so I can wash my hands and say the blessing. No more sleeping, no more dreaming. I lost half my life during the night."

"Get some more sleep," Matle said. "The shepherd hasn't yet blown the horn to drive his flock into the field."

"Oh no," Falik replied, "I wouldn't go back to sleep now for all the money in the world! If you want to sleep, sleep in good health! Just make sure that Shaya—may no good Jew have anything to do with him—doesn't come to you in a dream and snatch away some of your good health, the way he took away some of mine.

"He's got some nerve! As if it weren't enough for him to inflict such misery on me while I was awake during the day, he came to me in a dream and tortured me so badly that I don't know how I managed to survive. He even asked me to measure him. God in heaven, he should be measured for a shroud!"

Matle was soon back in bed and fast asleep. Falik went out into the courtyard to look around.

Never had he derived so much pleasure and joy from his house and courtyard as on this early morning after that terrifying dream. He wondered how he had been foolish enough to believe that he had sold his house. How could he possibly sell something that was dearer than life itself, something that he cherished more than all the delights in the world?

"Wise, wise, and yet a fool!" he told himself. "As soon as Shaya said the words 'sold your house,' you should have quickly realized that it was a dream, spit in his face, waited until you awoke, and not suffered any misery. And you, nitwit that you are, went ahead and believed him, and endured so much heartache, so much worry and grief!"

And he promised himself that next time, should Shaya come to him in a dream and ask to be measured, he would say right away, "Go, Reb Shaya, take part in someone else's dream, but don't come to me, because I will smash your skull with my pressing iron."

Falik went into the house, opened all the shutters, and sat down to work. His heart had still not stopped racing. He sewed as if in a trance, then put the work away and started to say the blessings. Putting on his prayer shawl and tefillin, he prayed so piously, so fervently, that he couldn't remember when he had ever poured out his heart to God with such devotion.

And the prayers fortified and soothed him. Putting away his prayer shawl and tefillin, he said to himself, "The world hasn't been abandoned yet. There is a God in heaven who doesn't allow the wealthy to swallow up His whole world as Shaya wants to do!"

This thought calmed him down completely, and Falik took up his work again. This time he sewed with new strength and spirit, just like in his younger days when he knew no worries and still believed that he was richer than anyone in the world.

Meanwhile, Matle rose too, said the blessing, heated the water, and handed Falik a fine glass of tea with milk and a fresh bagel. Falik felt happy and relaxed once again.

"Listen, Matle," he said to her contentedly, "a man is a fool if he worries, so long as he still has work! I just now accomplished in one stroke what, at another time, I probably wouldn't have accomplished in two days. I'm on my way to see Bunim to fit his overcoat and mark where to sew the buttons. You'll see, I'll deliver all the work by the holiday with His help, and we'll have an altogether joyous Shavuos.

"And listen, Matle, don't be stingy. Go ahead and bake those butter cakes, as only you can, and prepare coffee, like in the old days when we used to live so well!"

"God's mercy and your hard work, Husband," Matle replied. "I won't stint. If you'd always had such good sense, you'd have been a lot healthier."

Falik wrapped Bunim's coat in fabric and placed the bundle under his arm, but when he left the house to head towards Bunim's place, he saw several carts of bricks standing in the street. His heart sank, and again he felt an echo of that terrible misery he had suffered in his dream. He had the feeling that the drivers of the carts were waiting for Shaya to come to show them where to store the bricks in Falik's courtyard.

He went back into the house, looked for a lock, and bolted the gate. Returning to the house, he warned Matle, "Should Shaya come and want to stash his bricks in our yard, don't let him. Should he offer you money, even as much as a ruble a brick, spit in his face. Do you hear what I'm saying?"

"What, am I deaf?" asked Matle.

"Well, just don't be angry. I'll be right back."

"Go in good health!"

And once again, with the bundle under his arm, a needle and thread stuck in his lapel, and a piece of chalk in his pocket, Falik set off to Bunim's to fit his new overcoat.

CHAPTER SIX

THE SHAVUOS HOLIDAY was over, but Falik still had plenty of work.

"My enemies should have to do all their sewing alone without an assistant!" he complained to the householders whose garments had not been ready before the holiday or needed to be adjusted. They brought back clothing to be "taken in" or "let out," have buttons moved, a pocket sewn in, or other alterations promised for after the holiday.

"What can you do when you're punished by God, blessed be He, that you can't keep a decent worker these days? First of all, the impertinence of today's worker is not to be tolerated. And second, if you do find a good worker, off he goes to London or America, and try chasing after him!"

So he poured out his heart, sewing night and day, straining his old eyes during the entire week after the holiday just as he had the week before.

And construction began on Shaya's building.

Men returning from synagogue carrying their prayer shawl and tefillin bags under their arms stopped to watch the masons lay the foundation. They talked, pointed with their fingers, and argued with each other, just as if they knew a thing or two about what it took to build a house. Others, apparently with nothing better to do with their time, stood under Falik's window for hours on end, watching how they mixed lime with sand to make mortar. They showed off their expertise or offered all kinds of speculations and wild conjectures.

Falik watched it all through his window. He could hear those standing in the street saying, "Shaya is pouring gold into the foundation." And they all wished they could, at the very least, have in their pockets the cost of the foundation.

And Falik wanted to go out on the street, too, to take a closer look. Surely there was something worth watching. He felt as if tongs were pulling him outside to watch the masons at work.

Mixing into other people's affairs or attending someone's wedding or celebration as an uninvited guest are Jewish occupations. And what was Falik's soul, poor thing, if not a Jewish soul?

But Falik restrained himself, sat with his feet folded beneath him and sewed on, even though his heart and soul escaped across the street where workers carried bricks, laid stones, and sealed them with mortar. The building was just beginning to emerge from the ground.

"I mustn't keep this up!" he said to himself. "No one else will finish my work for me. Falik, in those good years, if a neighbor had put up a building across from your window, would you have just sat here? Would you have remained sitting inside the house and not been out there? But these are different times when a piece of clothing won't sew itself. Today,

Falik, in your misery, you simply can't allow yourself to indulge in such pleasures. Put up with your miserable problems and sew as long as there is something to sew! Alas, in the meantime, Shaya's house is going up without you. There's no point protesting."

Yet Falik was telling himself a lie. It wasn't the work that held him back. Somehow he would have found an excuse for himself and for the householders waiting for their garments. "What craftsman can be that punctual?" No, an entirely different reason kept him in the house and wouldn't let him go into the street, even though he did not want to admit it even to himself.

His heart screamed in turmoil, "Shaya Miller—may no good Jew have anything to do with him—has blocked the street and spoiled the pleasure I took in standing next to the building!"

Another time he told himself, "What are you worried about? You're as afraid of Shaya as of last year's snow. Do you, God forbid, owe him money? Or is he a governor-general that you have to fear him? Only in a dream could he have caused you such worry and heartache. Only in a dream could he have purchased your house. But to tell the truth, it's enough to make a cat laugh! On the contrary, what you'd like to do is show him that you don't care in the least, and should he try to bring even one load of bricks into your yard, it's the pressing iron to his head and the sewing shears to his stomach! That's how he'll know that a poor man also has the right not to let anyone take what's his against his will."

And as if to show Shaya that he wasn't afraid of him, Falik got up from his workbench, threw something over his shoulders, and boldly ran out to take a look at Shaya's building. But before he could get close, he caught sight of Shaya, who stood next to the workers from early morning until evening. And Falik said to himself, "The devil take him! Let him just try to start up with me. I don't want to have any dealings with him. What good would it do me?"

Discouraged, he returned home, threw off his top layer, and remained in his fringed undershirt and trousers. Sitting back down to sew, he grumbled a bit, perhaps with anger, perhaps with pride.

And so a few weeks passed, and Falik had less work to do. He barely had enough tailoring and alterations to fill a few hours each day, and Shaya's building was already well out of the ground. Through his window, Falik could see the first rows of bricks above the foundation.

He knew, of course, that watching from his window and standing on the street close to the building were as far apart as day from night, but did he have a choice? After all, Shaya Miller had become very distasteful to him, sticking like a bone in his throat. Rather than meet him face to face, it was better to simply look through the window from afar. That would have to do.

But to what lengths such a wicked man will go! Early one morning, Falik observed the workers digging ditches, putting in posts, and nailing boards to them. A fence to shield the building during construction!

Falik didn't imagine for a minute that the police had required Shaya to install the fence to protect passersby from falling bricks. He didn't really know, but was sure that Shaya had built the fence specifically to spite him. That way, he couldn't see them construct the house through his window, and feast his eyes even briefly.

"This man is evil, an enemy, may his name be erased!" Falik complained to Matle. "You see what someone stuffed full of Korach's fortune is capable of doing? Does he think I'm going to give his building the evil eye, or who knows what? So he goes and puts up a fence out of spite! It's as if he's saying, 'I thumb my nose at you, Falik. Look through your window as much as you want, you won't see a thing!'"

"May Shaya not be able to see out into the world," Matle exclaimed. "Why doesn't he stick to his own knitting? You'll be left with nothing if you can't watch them lay bricks. On the other hand, Husband, maybe it's for the best. Less dust will come into the house, and we can open a window. Ever since they began laying bricks, I sweep and sweep but can't manage to get the place clean. They should build him a grave in the cemetery already, God Almighty!"

"She doesn't understand. She's a foolish old woman," Falik said to himself. "Just try making her understand that I want to take a look, that it feels like tongs are pulling me to see a house like that develop."

Another time, Falik looked through his window at the fence, counted the boards, and thought, "Master of the Universe, why do you give one person everything, and the other, nothing? You know, of course, that I was once quite jealous of Shaya's money and his new building. Do you see those few boards that Shaya used for the fence out of spite? Were you to give them to me, I would praise you and thank you. It's a fine little pile of boards, more than enough to cover my roof. It would be nice, Master of the Universe, if you would send me a similar stack of boards, so I could rip out my rotten roof and lay a new one. Shaya's eyes would pop out of his head, and his fat stomach would split in fury. Tit for tat! You conceal your building with a fence so that I can't see the construction, and I show you that I have no intention of selling my house to you. Behold, I am making a new roof. Take a look and burst!"

And the taller Shaya's building grew, the more Falik's heart sank. He could barely figure out for himself why he hated Shaya so much.

"There's nothing to lose," he had said to Shaya when he wanted to buy a few pieces of his old lumber. "How dare Shaya even propose that I sell him my house?"

Falik asked himself this question from time to time. He didn't want to think ill of Shaya, but couldn't stop himself.

"Shaya is making my life miserable," Falik told himself. "Shaya's whole purpose with the building, with the fence in front of the building, and with all of his hanging around here, is just so that he can spy on my house. The whole world isn't enough for him, but he won't succeed with me."

And it seemed to Falik that his house became a little poorer, lonelier, and altogether more depressed because of the new neighbor Shaya was putting up across the way. And Falik wanted to console his house, tell him not to feel downhearted in his poverty.

He did not admit to himself that he, too, felt downhearted and discouraged because of his own poverty.

CHAPTER SEVEN

THE WORKERS CONSTRUCTING Shaya's house often came into Falik's kitchen. A few for a drink of water and a few to warm up dinner in a pot on Falik's stove. Sometimes Falik would ask them, "How are things? How far along is the building?" or "What's Shaya up to?" And from them, he discovered that Shaya hadn't come around to check on his building for two or three days. Even the workers didn't know why he had stopped coming. Falik began to question Shaya's Jewish clerks, who told him that Shaya had recently taken ill. The fat from his big belly had oozed into his heart, probably from the excessive heat, and his physician had sent him off to the thermal baths to have the fat sucked out of his big stomach.

Quite pleased, Falik asked, "When will he be back?"

"Hopefully by Shabbes Nachamu or for the High Holidays."

"Only a rich man can afford to indulge himself like that," Matle remarked. "Putting up a building like this here, and he himself going off to the baths."

Falik didn't see any reason to express an opinion now that Shaya was gone and he was rid of him for a good two months. "Now, who cares what Shaya thinks!" he said to himself. And not waiting an extra minute, he raced out to inspect what had been done and how the construction was going.

And inspect Falik did, just as it should be inspected. Not in passing, like everyone else, but like a starving man grabs food after a long fast, he jumped in with both feet to examine everything. And he didn't notice that half a day had passed, and there in his own house, he had left his work scattered about and hadn't even taken the time to finish the piece he was working on.

"Falik, Falik!" he suddenly heard Matle calling him through the window. "A customer has come and brought a little work." Reluctantly, Falik tore himself away from the pleasure of watching the construction and went back into the house.

Matle met him in the vestibule and pointed out that his hat, coat, and vest were sprayed with whitewash, and his boots were covered in clay dust like a mason's. "Just look at you! Where have you been crawling around?"

Falik couldn't help but be ashamed when he saw how he was covered in dust and lime. "No harm done," he answered Matle. "At least I was able to see it all."

"But let me dust you off and clean you up a little, pleaded Matle. "I'm embarrassed in front of the customer!"

But Falik quickly tore into the dining room to measure the customer and get rid of him. He wanted to hurry out to the building where he still had things to look over and questions to ask so he could get detailed explanations about what wasn't yet clear.

Matle ran after him with the clothes brush, dusting off his back and shoulders.

"Today is Tuesday, Reb Falik," said the customer. "Take my measurements, sit down to sew, and have it ready for Shabbes."

"Everybody wants it for Shabbes!" Falik retorted, sounding none too happy. "Do you think an artisan can whip it out just like that? Everything you see lying on the table, they also want for Shabbes."

"If you want to, Reb Falik, I'm sure you'll figure it out. After all, I'm a longtime customer."

"If you don't believe me, what can I do for you?" replied Falik. "By all means, advise me how to be fair to the others as well?"

"My advice is: take less of an interest in Shaya's building. Don't waste your time standing around for hours in the middle of the day watching them lay bricks."

"Indeed, it's just like everyone says," answered Falik. " 'When you cry, no one sees. When you laugh, everyone sees.' Why didn't you notice that the whole time they've been building, I have sat, hunched over like a hook, and haven't gone out to look even once?"

"Who stopped you?"

"You mean, no doubt, that Shaya didn't let me?" Falik blurted out, just as if the other knew what was in his heart. "That makes me laugh! Why should I be afraid of him? It just so happens that I was up to my neck in work and couldn't get out."

Falik measured the customer, jotted something down in his notebook, and thought he'd finally get rid of him. Instead, the fellow just took a seat and said he wasn't leaving until Falik cut the material right there in front of him. That way, he'd at least know that Falik would sit down to sew it right away and have it done by Shabbes.

In order to rid himself of this troublesome nuisance, Falik took up his scissors, ruler, and chalk and cut out the material before the customer's eyes. That didn't help either. The customer was one of those older proprietors whose wives sit in their shops watching the buyers. The men search out places to pass an hour or so as a way of shortening a long day.

He consequently took to asking Falik what his sons wrote from America. And when Falik answered him tersely, he began to fill him in about his own children. Falik thought he was going to pass out. All he wanted was to free himself and get back to Shaya's building.

"What a stroke of bad luck!" he said to himself, quite angry. "A new Shaya on my back!"

The customer didn't leave until afternoon prayers. Between afternoon and evening prayers, Falik slipped out again and was at least able to see how the foreman explained to the workers what to do early the next morning before his arrival. For that, however, Falik sewed late into the night.

In vain Matle reminded him, "Falik, it's not just before a holiday now. It's a shame to waste the kerosene. You can finish all this work during the day." But it did no good.

"She's a foolish old woman," he said to himself instead of answering her. "She hasn't the slightest notion about any of this. It's all the same to her whether they build a wooden shack or a three-story building where there's certainly something worth seeing. The customer doesn't care, so I've got to finish his clothing by Shabbes, even if I have to sit up all night."

The next day was the same. Falik divided his day between the work in his shop and the work on Shaya's building.

In the beginning, just the novelty of seeing the big building appear in the place of the old ruin was enough to have him stand for hours under the burning sun. While he watched, he didn't even remember the unfinished work in his house and the customers waiting for it.

Later, however, he began to comprehend how everything that was being done on the building was proceeding in a set order according to a plan that had been drafted beforehand. Now the work acquired a special charm that his head and intellect appreciated, and his heart, deep within, felt and enjoyed.

He had already gotten to know the ordinary workers. They called him "Neighbor" and let him climb freely onto the scaffolding, and even stand next to them on the wall as they worked. After a while, he became acquainted with the architect as well, and from him, Falik learned a lot about the construction process that the ordinary workers couldn't explain. Day by day, he became more knowledgeable, and Shaya's building occupied all his thoughts. He frittered away whole days like this.

"Good heavens, Falik, what are you thinking?" Matle once challenged him. "Who has ever heard of a person spending all day at someone else's building site? I ask you, how is this not a disgrace before God and before other people—not to mention for yourself? A customer brings a bit of work, or you're called to someone's house to take a measurement—you're never at home. 'Where is Reb Falik?' they ask. Go tell them a story that in his old age Reb Falik is done being a tailor and is helping Shaya Miller build his house!

"And do you think the customers don't see you over there on the scaffold? 'What's your husband doing way up there?' they ask and point their fingers at you."

Falik paid some heed. He felt that Matle was right, but after all, she was a foolish old woman! She didn't know the first thing about it, and he couldn't make her understand how he felt standing on the scaffold watching them lay bricks.

"And I'd like to know, what do you get out of it?" Matle continued to grumble. "From this, do you get good health? Does anything go into your pocket? Or maybe Shaya pays you a wage to oversee how they build his house?

"Shaya must have put you under some sort of magic spell, heaven forbid. From the first minute when he turned up here to build his house, you haven't been the same person you were. Why don't you say anything? Why don't you answer me?"

Falik heard out her complaint like a child listening to his mother lecture him. "Do you think, Matle, that tailoring is the only trade there is?" he exclaimed in spite of himself. "You should know that building a house according to a plan is also a craft. A major craft, I tell you! And it involves a great intelligence. And the nature of a great intelligence is it raises you up. It simply helps you see and understand everything better. Do you understand what's being said to you?"

Chapter Eight

THE ENTIRE TIME Falik was so involved in Shaya's building, he almost forgot about Shaya altogether. It was as if the house built itself without a boss, without any direction from a Shaya or anybody else. It built itself because construction was by its nature an intelligent craft and the work had a flavor that was enough to make it worthwhile. So what if Matle shouted? She was a foolish woman! In truth, how could she know the appeal of construction? Construction was a man's business and not an affair for a woman who wouldn't know the first thing about it.

But now began the three weeks before Tishah b'Av. Bit by bit, work began to appear for the tailors in the town. To Falik, as well, people brought in pieces of cloth to be sewn for Shabbes Nachamu. Matle did not let Falik waste any time and rarely stepped away from the sewing table. But, no sooner had she become occupied in the kitchen or was off shooing away the cat from a piece of meat on the draining board than Falik dashed outside, often just as he was in his fringed woolen under-shirt with his tape measure over his shoulders. And before Matle had a chance to even look around, he was up on the highest scaffold next to the masons.

But it wasn't long before he heard Matle's voice calling out to him, "Falik, Falik! You are to come back into the house this very instant. Are you listening?"

And like a schoolboy making mischief with his friends in the yard who is called back to class by the rebbe, Falik reluctantly returned to his workshop, mumbling to himself, "Everything just to put food in your belly! Sit all day all hunched over like a hook and just sew and sew some more! Nobody understands that a tailor also has a soul and eyes in his head. Even a tailor can see and enjoy what is intelligent and beautiful."

During one of those moments when his Matle was busy with something in the kitchen or courtyard, Falik stood on the scaffold and carefully investigated a question left from the day before. Suddenly he felt someone grab hold of the edge of the tape measure hanging over his shoulders.

"How are you, Reb Falik?"

He looked around and saw—Shaya! The same Shaya as far as his face was concerned, but of his stomach, barely a third remained.

"It looks like the warm baths weren't a joke! They must have drained off thirty-five pounds of fat," thought Falik, and in the same moment, an image appeared of Fat Shaya standing in an overheated steam bath with his stomach hanging out. The doctor twists a faucet into his stomach, either brass or copper. Shaya the Pig would be too stingy to splurge on silver! The doctor places a pot below, turns on the tap, and the fat begins to pour out of Shaya's stomach like olive oil from a barrel.

"Serves him right!" thought Falik. "Someone like that shouldn't think he can swallow up the whole world in his fat self!"

"What, Falik, you're still angry with me?" Shaya asked with a friendly smile.

"What's this about angry?" Falik answered, somewhat embarrassed. "I have to say, you didn't do anything to me, and what could you do to me, anyway?"

"And I truly never wished to do you any harm, God forbid!" Shaya assured him. "I never wanted to, and I still don't want to buy your house. What I have is enough, thank God! I became quite ill and had to spend more than two months out of the country. And do you think I feel perfectly well now? I feel useless, I tell you."

For some reason, this conversation touched Falik's heart. Someone completely different from the Shaya in his dream spoke to him now and assured him that he never had any intention of buying his house.

"And what are you doing up here on the scaffolding, Reb Falik?" asked Shaya. "Do you want to take the measurements of the house perhaps, or maybe of one of the workmen?"

"Not at all," replied Falik. "I popped over for a minute just to take a quick look."

As he began to climb down, Shaya held him back. "It's a good thing I ran into you here," Shaya said. "Seeing the measuring tape hanging from your shoulders reminds me that, as it happens, I need to take in the clothes that are too big for me now. Even though Shloyme the Tailor has always done my work, we're going to be neighbors soon, God willing, so I prefer you, Reb Falik. I'd like you to come home with me to take my measurements. Take the clothes that are worth altering, and do them as quickly as you can."

Falik began to scratch his neck as if he were wrestling with the question, "Go or not go?"

"With a close neighbor, one has to live in peace, Reb Falik," said Shaya. "Peace is a precious thing, and I hope you will have a lot of work from my house."

"I'll come by in about an hour," Falik finally said decisively. "Good day to you in the meantime."

"So long. I'll expect you, Reb Falik!" Shaya shouted after him.

And when Matle jumped all over him to scold him for crawling around on the scaffolding again, this time Falik answered her proudly, "You see—a person doesn't take any steps without good reason. Had I not been there, I would certainly not have acquired such a valuable customer. Shaya asked me to go to his place to alter the clothes that are ready at present, and promised me work from his house from now on. You should have seen him, Matle. He wasn't at all the same Shaya. There isn't any trace of his fat stomach."

An hour later, Falik was already at Shaya's to take his measurements, and returned home with a big bundle of clothing to be altered. Falik soon sat down to work and sewed with enthusiasm. He didn't want to get off on the wrong foot.

"Let him know that what I, Falik, have already forgotten, the other tailors in town should come learn from me!" he told himself with spirit.

As he worked, Falik wondered, "Why did I once detest this same Shaya so much? I simply couldn't bear hearing his name mentioned, and why has the hatred disappeared altogether? And I definitely want the clothes that I am altering to fit perfectly.

"It's no wonder," he explained his bewilderment to himself. "Before, this same Shaya was like a stuffed barrel. No waist, not much of a physique. Maybe you could sew a sack for that kind of person. Now that he's allowed the fat to be sucked out, however, he has a nice physique. His shoulders are shoulders, and his waist is a waist. A fine figure of a man. So now I can look at him and actually sew for him."

CHAPTER NINE

FOR A FULL WEEK, Falik was busy with Shaya's garments. He took such pains to do a good job that he almost forgot about Shaya's building and didn't leave the workshop even once to see how things were going.

When Falik delivered the carefully altered clothing, Shaya called his wife in to judge how they fit.

"Hassia, do you know who this is?"

"I don't know Reb Falik?" answered Shaya's wife. "What, am I not from here that you have to ask?"

"That's not what I mean," Shaya replied. "I just mean to say that it's our good luck that Reb Falik is a very close neighbor of the new house. Therefore, it's only right that you offer him a small glass of brandy. What do you say, Hassia, is Reb Falik a good craftsman?"

"As good as they come!" answered Hassia, quite satisfied that the clothing fit her husband as if made to measure. "They fit better than when they were new."

"Don't you think so, Reb Falik?" Shaya turned to him satisfied and with a friendly smile.

"If your wife says so, you may believe her," replied Falik. "It wouldn't do for me to praise my own work. And if you don't believe your Hassia, go out on the street. You'll hear what people will say."

"Why do I need to hear what people say if I can tell on my own that it's good?" Shaya asked. "How much do I owe you for this work, Reb Falik?"

Falik gave it some thought, calculated in his head, and said, "So as not to haggle, Reb Shaya, I think ten would be fair."

"For ten rubles, Shloyme the Tailor would also have done the job," Shaya's wife exclaimed.

"Would you have been more impressed if Shloyme had done it?" Falik asked. "If you were to look closely, this same Shloyme, with his big master workshop and ten journeymen, was actually my own journeyman! He learned the trade from me, and, not to boast, as far as I'm concerned, I could still teach him a thing or two."

"But what kind of talk is this?" Shaya scolded his wife. "You know that I don't like you to haggle over wages. And with a future neighbor, God willing, I certainly don't want to dicker. If Reb Falik says ten, then it's ten! I'm more than happy to give it to him because I am pleased with his work."

With these words, Shaya took a ten ruble note out of his pocket and handed it to Falik.

"Wear it in good health!" Falik said, wishing him well. Then taking a look at Hassia, he thought, "It's about time for her to visit the thermal baths to drain the fat. But this time, it would be pure pig fat. I can see the pig on her face."

"Hassia, didn't I say let's have a little brandy?" Shaya called out to his wife, who had stormed away when her husband gave Falik the ten rubles without bargaining.

"I thank you, Reb Shaya, but it isn't necessary. I haven't had a drink in quite a while. Really, there's no need. Have yourself a good day!" said Falik, turning to leave.

"No! First, I'd like to drink to the clothing," said Shaya. "And second, to properly renew our neighborly friendship with a good-sized glass of liquor. Wait a minute, I'll be right back."

Against his will, Falik was forced to wait, and Shaya brought in a bottle. The maid placed the glasses on the table. Shaya asked her to bring something to nibble on, poured two big glasses, and said to Falik, "So, Reb Falik, don't wait to be asked. Have a drink."

"You have the first glass," said Falik.

"I've just come from Marienbad, Reb Falik, and can't drink. The doctor warned me: keep to your diet for another six weeks or so. That means not to eat the wrong foods, and no liquor should pass my lips."

"L'chaim!" said Falik. "We should have the honor of drinking at your housewarming, Reb Shaya!"

"Amen!" answered Shaya, and Falik drained his glass to the very last drop.

"It's been a long time since I've had such strong brandy," sputtered Falik.

"So, and now for me!" said Shaya. "I'll say, 'L'chaim,' and you do the honors."

In his younger years, Falik, like all craftsmen, had nothing against liquor, especially when he had delivered a piece of work to a patron, and it was the patron who treated. But now he was afraid that Shaya would get him all befuddled. He tried to refuse. Shaya, however, did not give up, and Falik was forced to drink Shaya's glass as well, right down to the bottom.

"This is to celebrate that we are neighbors, Reb Falik! Now let's drink to your craftsmanship."

"Let me be, Reb Shaya," begged Falik. "It feels as if the brandy is already creeping into my head. In old age, that's no trifling matter."

But it didn't do any good. Shaya wouldn't take no for an answer. Falik must drink again, must have at least one in honor of the clothing.

"Unless you don't want to work for me any longer, Reb Falik," Shaya said.

Falik reluctantly downed a third glass and certainly didn't need any more. His eyes narrowed, his feet felt like wooden blocks that wouldn't budge.

"Now have a bite of something," Shaya insisted.

Falik put something in his mouth, and Shaya saw that now was the time to bring up selling the house again.

"In short, you'd like to live out your years under your own roof," Shaya began as if picking up in the middle of a conversation. "That's no sin! But of what use is that ruin to you? With the money I'd give you for your land, you could build a new house that would really be something to see on a different street.

"Do you know why I'm so interested? Are there not other houses and properties to buy in town? There are plenty, and certainly many bigger and more attractive than yours. And maybe even for half the price that I'm offering you, but my interest is this: If you sell me your property, I'll transfer my mill over here. There, where my mill is now, I'm thinking of constructing an oil press. So for that reason, it's worth it to me to give you a few hundred rubles extra."

Falik, who at first didn't have the slightest idea what Shaya was talking about, suddenly felt a bitterness and sadness in his heart that reminded him of his dream. He wanted to reply with anger, with resentment, but it was as if his lips were frozen. He muttered something, but neither Shaya nor even he himself could make out what his tongue was babbling.

"May God punish me, Reb Falik, if I mean to force you, or even to talk you into something that isn't better for you," Shaya swore, offering Falik his hand. "But you should know, in order to consult with your wife and your son-in-law with a clear head . . .

"What a fine young man, your son-in-law! I like him and often lend him a hundred rubles interest-free. But that isn't what I want to say. What I mean is this: You yourself must have the good sense to understand that if I give you fifteen hundred rubles for your house, no one else will match that price. So be it, if you're not interested, it's your choice! But give me your word that if you should, indeed, want to sell sometime, you won't mention it to any other buyer without letting me know first. It's not a sin to ask, in my opinion."

Falik sat, his heart sinking, his thoughts muddled and racing around in his head. But he'd lost his tongue. He was overcome and afraid to utter a word.

"Do you promise?" Shaya asked again.

"Yes!" answered Falik, just to get rid of him.

He quickly picked himself up and barely managed to come out with "Good day!" as he left the house.

In the fresh air, his tongue loosened, and Falik began to curse Shaya's ancestors under his breath.

"The Evil Inclination itself! Satan sowing confusion, may his name be blotted out!" he muttered. He tripped over his own feet and felt as if he was struggling to go uphill. He sensed that he was drunk but was certain that his reason hadn't been affected in the least. In order to check whether he still had the ten rubles, he reached into his pocket and squeezed the paper tightly. He could feel it in his hand but still didn't believe it. He tried to recalculate: How had the total for the work come to a whole ten rubles?

He figured it out and remembered everything accurately.

"That means," he told himself, "I haven't drowned my brains in drink and can safely say that I haven't agreed to sell him my house.

"If I want to sell my house, should I let him know before anyone else? To that, I said 'yes.' He's been sick for so long, and that wife of his! She's somewhat of a shady lady, a stuffed hog! They should draw her blood, not her fat! I hate her seven times more than I hate Shaya. Shaya has some shape, has a figure. If you make an effort, you can sew him an outfit that looks good on him. She's a clumsy oaf!

"Thank God I am not a ladies tailor and don't have to sew for the likes of her. I am not in the least jealous of Shaya that he has such a wife. I wouldn't trade my Matle's foot for any part of her. A tub of lard! Draining wouldn't even help!"

"Reb Falik? What's this?" said a nearby voice. Looking around, he recognized one of his tenants.

"What's the occasion for such a big celebration today?" remarked the tenant. "You look a little tipsy, Reb Falik!"

"A little bit of an occasion, yes, a ceremony for tailors."

"And what does that mean?"

"That means, when we have a new client, we bring him a completed piece of work. That's a tailors' celebration. Do you see what I mean?"

"Is this the first time you've delivered a piece of merchandise? Why have I never seen you in such high spirits before?"

"It's all right! Believe me, I'm not guilty!" Falik swore. "Shaya Miller insisted. Another glass and another glass. At first, I didn't understand what he wanted. Soon, however, he revealed what he had in mind. But so long as my head doesn't continue to ache, he won't get his way."

"So what does he want?" the tenant asked.

"He wants . . . Better not to repeat it!" Turning to his tenant, Falik said, "However, I beg you, don't say anything to my Matle. She'll worry. A pity, she's a dear woman, my Matle, may she live to be a hundred and twenty!"

"And are you really afraid that your Matle will divorce you if she finds out that Shaya got you drunk?" asked the tenant in jest.

"Afraid? Certainly not. My Matle is not the kind of woman a husband has to fear. But I want to spare her the heartache. Do you understand?"

"What kind of business do you have with Shaya?" the tenant wanted to know.

"You want to know everything! You will become old before your time."

"A secret matter?" the tenant pressed him.

"What kind of secret? I brought over a piece of work. He's satisfied. He offered me something to drink, something to eat. That's all there is to it! He just came back from the thermal baths. They must have drained away thirty-five pounds of fat.

Now he has a fine figure, and one can sew for him. No wonder he's pleased. But his other half! I am not jealous. What a tub of lard. Pure lard, and just as unkosher. A despicable woman. I hate her! But what concern is it of yours?"

As Falik moved on, he addressed his stumbling feet, "How does this affect you more than the head on my shoulders? I surely did not expect to live to see this from you. Hey! We're on our way. Get going, what's taking so long? Get a move on!"

Approaching his house, he thought it seemed to sway and dance for joy.

"Oh, it's not seemly for such an old-timer to be drunk!" he said to the house. "If you knew what Shaya Miller thinks of you, you wouldn't be dancing. Hateful, brother, hateful!"

At that, Matle spotted him through the window and ran out to meet him. Seeing her husband drunk, perhaps for the first time since their wedding, she screamed, "Heaven help me! Falik, you are drunk! Woe is me that I have lived to see this!"

"Here, see if I'm tipsy!" he answered with the courage of a drunk. "I've just brought you ten rubles! Maybe you think I have no idea where I am? It's just that my feet became weak, Matle. My head, however, is as strong as can be. Just let Shaya try to trick me. No matter how long he keeps humiliating me, he won't succeed."

"Come inside, at least, so I won't be so ashamed," Matle cried and dragged him in by his sleeve.

Falik tripped on the threshold, staggered, and fell. Terrified, Matle tried to lift him off the floor.

"Away!" he shouted. "I fell on my own, I'll pick myself up on my own!"

But Matle didn't let go. She hoisted him up and led him to the bed.

"Nice, very nice! Here is something to make me proud!" Matle lamented and started to cry. "If Toybele sees this, she'll bury herself alive for shame! If the boys in America hear about it, they'll be embarrassed to go out in the street and show themselves in public! Their father a drunk! Look how easily that rolls off my tongue. Woe is me! Who could have imagined this? Why did I have to live to see this?"

Matle's tears soon had an effect on Falik. He, too, burst into tears and sobbed like a small child.

Matle wanted to calm him, but Falik's heart was too worked up. He finally fell into a deep sleep and slept that way right through afternoon prayers, evening prayers, and supper, until early the next morning.

When he went outside onto the street and saw his house, he felt terribly guilty. Guilty that he had taken an interest in nothing but Shaya's house for two months and hardly given his own house a thought. Guilty, too, that his house, his poor lonely house, had seen him so merry and drunk the previous day, and was certainly ashamed of its owner.

"You've lived to see your owner drunk in the middle of the week, on a Wednesday no less!" he said to the house. "Are you ashamed of me? Make no mistake, good brother. Shaya the Thief wanted to get you drunk and knock you off your feet, not me. I benefited on your behalf, so to speak, and now I'm ashamed to look my own Matle in the eye!"

Before going back inside, he added, "Anyway, don't worry about a thing, my friend. The wisest man might do something foolish once, but never again. Never again! Ugh, I have such a bad taste in my mouth. I tell you, it's as if I had poison in my stomach!"

Chapter Ten

ALONG WITH SOBERING UP after Shaya's brandy, Falik also over-
came his obsession with Shaya's building. He now realized and
freely admitted to Matle that she had been right all along and
was certainly right now.

"To tell the truth, Matle," he told her, "a little liquor is a
good thing, really. You take a drop, and your heart soars. But
one drop leads to another, and then another. To get drunk in
the middle of a Wednesday, and to be so humiliated! Staring at
a beautiful building isn't really a sin, but it is a temptation!
You neglect what's yours for the sake of something that belongs
to someone else. I've barely glanced at my own house and yard
in the past two months, and they've both rotted a little more.
The fence leans as if it's saying 'we bend the knee' in prayer.
The steps in the cellar are broken and neglected. Serves me
right! Hammer and nails won't even help now. But what hurts
the most is the roof. Good heavens, the roof! I don't begin to
know how we'll get through the winter under this tattered
skullcap!"

"Don't worry, Husband," Matle consoled him. "Take up your
work again, and trust in God. You'll see—He'll take care of us
yet."

"But the boys don't even take the trouble to answer our letter," Falik said. "Look, their papa hardly asks them for anything, and they don't write a word."

"Maybe they didn't, maybe they couldn't. One mustn't judge a child!" their loyal mother defended them.

And Falik got back to work. During the month of Elul, every tailor has plenty to occupy him, and Falik too had no less work than other years at this time. He still wanted to slip out for just a minute to see them finish Shaya's house. How would they construct the cornices up above, install the rafters, and then cover the roof with tin? But no! He dreaded running into Shaya even more than before.

Before, he simply hated him but wasn't frightened of him. Now, although he didn't hate Shaya at all, he was suddenly afraid of him.

It occurred to Falik that he did owe Shaya something. Shaya had spoken to him, not the way a rich man speaks to a craftsman who delivers some work, but plainly, the way a householder speaks to another householder, a neighbor to a neighbor. Shaya gave him a ten ruble note for the work, as he requested, and didn't try to knock off a single ruble the way other householders would. And though Shaya's brandy had shamed him before his own wife and house, Shaya did what was right and wasn't stingy at Falik's expense. He, Falik, needed to understand that if one person felt obliged to ask, the other shouldn't lose all sense of proportion.

And Falik felt that Shaya had acquired some sort of power over him, which he couldn't begin to explain even to himself. A power that paralyzed his tongue and took away his speech and energy. It seemed to Falik that if Shaya only wanted to, he could mold him like wax and fashion him into . . . whatever he wanted.

He could sense Shaya's power the night of his terrible dream. He could sense it as he sat confused at Shaya's house in a drunken fog where he had remained silent even though his heart was bursting to answer, "I'd sooner let you buy my life than my house!"

And looking out the window, whenever he spotted Shaya arriving at his building, a chill passed through his bones. He only felt it ease when Shaya left.

"No, no!" Falik often said to himself, protesting against the power he felt Shaya had over him. "I owe him nothing, nothing, not even a groschen! He gave me ten rubles. Haven't I earned them fair and square? He spoke to me like I was an equal, like a neighbor. Am I not a Jew, the grandson of Abraham Our Father, just as he is? Is he wealthier than I am? A lie! He just has more money than I do, but I am richer! I wouldn't trade my Matle's foot for his wife's head. He wants to swallow up the whole world, and all I want is a new roof over my house.

"No, I am not afraid of him. He won't manage to get me drunk a second time!" And he pierced the fabric firmly and quickly with his needle and struggled to chase the unpleasant thoughts from his head.

And time did not stand still. The holidays were approaching, the days were shorter, and one day Falik suddenly realized that Shaya's building was blocking half his light.

He consoled himself: It'll only be like this as long as the new house is hidden by scaffolding. As soon as they take the scaffolding down, I won't lack for light in my window.

But his roof was a bigger worry. The High Holidays brought the rainy autumn season, and he strongly doubted the old roof could withstand that test and keep the rain out of the house.

"Children, children!" he said to himself. "Surely they'll send something. I'm as sure of that as of myself. Good children, devoted children. But still, they're children. They have no idea how I wear myself out waiting, and the house definitely can't wait!"

And although he was certain that the children would send money for a new roof, still he pushed himself and strained his old eyes working late into the night. Even if they didn't send anything, he'd be able to save a few rubles from his holiday earnings. At least he'd be able to board up the holes a little and manage to get through the winter.

And Matle also skimped. She had even less hope than her husband that they would receive help from the children and knew very well why the few groschen they were able to set aside were needed now.

On Rosh Hashanah and Yom Kippur, the weather was actually beautiful and dry. Therefore, as was customary, it rained all through Sukkos. Falik sat with his tenants in the sukkah. No sooner had the rain started coming down in buckets than they all ran for the house, plates in hand. How Falik's heart sank, poor soul, when he saw that inside the house, it rained on him and his tenants no less than in the sukkah.

"Landlord," joked one of the tenants. "Let's go back into the sukkah! It's worse inside the house."

"He pours salt on my wounds!" Falik muttered under his breath.

"What now, Landlord?" the tenant shouted loudly. "Not in the sukkah and not in the house. Maybe we should just crawl underground?"

"It's the holiday, after all. I'm not going to clamber up on the roof to fix it on a holiday!" Falik replied. "If we get a little rain, we'll set out a few pans. What else can a Jew do on a holiday?"

And poor Jewish tenants are already used to setting down a pot or a bucket when it rains in the street and drips on their heads inside.

Falik made it through the holiday without too much damage, all things considered, but it was even worse a week later on Shabbes Bereishis. And on Shabbes Noah, the whole flood poured down on Falik's ark.

"Gentlemen," Falik said to the tenants the following day. "You want it to stop raining in the house, right? Pay me what you owe for this month's rent, plus a ruble for the next six months in advance. I'll also collect what my customers owe me. Putting everything together, I'll be able to patch up the roof. What choice do I have? America is so far, and autumn already so close! And I don't want to wait until the children remember to send their father a new roof."

"Don't think for a minute, Reb Falik, that a few patches are going to help your roof! What will hold the nails? It's all rot and spider webs. If you can install a new roof, go ahead! If not, we'll move out and not give you a groschen for rent, not even for the current month!" So announced Beryl the Coachman on his own behalf and on behalf of the other two tenants who resided with him in Falik's house.

Falik went ahead and consulted workmen anyway, but they told him the same thing: There was nothing to be done for the old roof. They would have to lay a new roof from start to finish.

Falik still didn't lose hope. After all, the children were sure to send money. They must send it and they would! And every time he saw the postman, Falik ran to ask if he had a letter for him from America.

Finally, one day out of the blue, the postman came in with a letter. But before giving it to him, he asked for a payment of twenty kopeks and showed him the small stamp on the envelope with the number twenty.

Falik had a hard time understanding why he had to pay twenty kopeks. It looked like the letter already had three stamps. Wasn't there a limit? The mail carrier had to explain long and hard before Falik accepted it. Matle had just gone to the butcher's, and Falik didn't have a groschen to his name.

He turned to one of the tenants who had just come inside to be present when Falik read the letter from America. "Lend me twenty kopeks until Matle gets back," Falik begged. But the tenant was afraid Falik would keep the twenty kopeks as rent money, which was already a month late, and refused to give it to him.

"Foolish man," said Falik to the tenant with pride and confidence. "Why are you afraid? You can surely see that a roof for the house lies here in this letter. Quickly, let me see already how much they've sent and how they're doing."

The tenant also thought that there must be money or a bank draft in the letter. Otherwise, the postman wouldn't have asked for a whole twenty kopeks. And this time, he took a chance and trusted Falik with the coins.

With trembling hands, Falik opened the letter.

There was no money and no draft.

Falik smoothed out the letter, poked around in the empty envelope, and searched on the ground in case the draft had accidentally fallen out. Nothing!

"Not a thing. They didn't send any money!" observed the tenant to get back at Falik, who had, in the meantime, tricked him out of twenty kopeks.

"If you count on children, you'll always be disappointed," observed the tenant who occupied the kitchen. She was a widow with children somewhere in America who barely remembered to write her once a year.

Falik braced himself and began to read. And in the letter, the children wrote that they had had a very good summer. Shloymke was about to be married, and Chaimke also had an eye on a bride. In short, they were all going to make a good life in America.

In regard to their father's request that they send him money for a new roof for his "old ruin," they were obliged to say that they found that their brother-in-law, Toybele's husband, was much more practical than he, their father. According to their brother-in-law, their father could get fifteen hundred rubles for the little house.

That the house was already in ruins, they could figure out just from their father's letter. Therefore, it would be a pity to spend even one groschen on a new roof. It would be better to sell the hovel as is, take the money, give Toybele five hundred rubles, and keep the rest. He and their mother should then come to America and not have to spend their lives lonely and worried.

"In America, Papa," the elder son added, "children toil for their parents, and not parents for their children!"

You've worked hard enough for us already. Now it's our turn to work hard on your behalf!

You and Mama come stay with us. It will be the best of all possible worlds, and you won't be in the way. If you don't want to live with us, you'll have your thousand rubles. It's only worth five hundred dollars here, but it will be enough for you to rent an apartment with good furniture. At the very worst, Papa, you can establish yourself with a thousand times more security than at home.

In America, you don't even have to be a master craftsman. Twenty workers deal with one garment: one cuts, another bastes, a third stitches on the machine, and so on. Even someone who can do nothing but sew buttons properly earns more than the specialist tailor where you are.

We beg you and Mother. Don't think of doing anything else. See about getting rid of your old shack as quickly as you can, pack up your bags and baggage, and come!

You don't have to worry about us, Papa. You aren't in any way obliged to leave us a house with an intact roof. In any case, we will not return to our old home. It's best if everyone from the old home comes to us, rather than we come to you. According to what we read in the local newspapers and what we hear, things are getting worse and worse for our brothers where you are. Why should you wait until they chase you out with sticks, God forbid? Better to leave on your own.

It's a free world here. Jewish or not Jewish, everyone is equal. And parents with adult children don't have to dread old age.

Toybele and her husband will come as well, and there's nothing to discuss. The old walls, the rotten roof, useless to us all! And when you come here, Papa, you'll finally see the kinds of houses we have in America.

Write soon that you have sold the house. We'll send steamship tickets for you and Mama and let you know what arrangements to make.

We hope to see you soon in America in good health!

* * * * *

"A precious letter, a thousand times more precious than a new roof over your house, Reb Falik!" observed his tenant when Falik had finished reading the letter.

"You'd be a fool not to do as they say!" the second tenant offered his point of view. "The truth is, why worry what will happen after you reach your allotted hundred and twenty years? It's all the same whether you leave your children all of your property—or nothing at all!"

The lady tenant also had something to say, "Your children are gold, Reb Falik. You should thank God for such children! Here is my proof: I, too, have sons and daughters somewhere in the world. Do I know the least thing about them? I would crawl to them on all fours if I only knew where they were!"

At that, Matle arrived home.

"How your belly is blessed, dearest Matle!" exclaimed the lady tenant as she ran to tell her the joyful news about the letter. "Your husband just read us the mail that came to you from your children. Every word is like gold!"

Falik reread the letter to Matle. All the tenants heard it again, and when Falik finished it a second time, they all agreed, "May God, blessed be He, help your children for honoring their parents so!"

"Now what do you say?" Falik asked Matle.

"Do I know? Indeed, for their kind hearts and honoring their parents, may God reward our children with everything we wish for them!"

"What's true is true," Falik agreed. "They are certainly good children. But it's becoming clear that good as they are, a new roof won't come of it!"

Chapter Eleven

And Falik's head reeled from lack of sleep and worry about what would happen now. Yes, he had the urge to travel and see how his children lived in America. To spend a few weeks there to remind them that there is a God in the world who keeps an eye on America just as He does here, and that what is forbidden here is also forbidden in America. And at the same time, to behold cities, all kinds of peoples, seas and rivers, and everything else to look at in God's world.

"If only I could take a trip for a few weeks and then return to my town and still be the owner of my own house like before," he told himself. "But that's not what the children have in mind. They order us to sell the house, to uproot ourselves from our old home, to move all the way over there and remain in America forever.

"No! That I cannot do," he often muttered under his breath. And he sat hunched over in his shop, his hands busily stitching away, and his head endlessly mulling it over.

"I tell you, Matle," he said to his wife as he sewed, "reading their letter was painful. They want us to live out our remaining years there, near them. Very nice of them, but I'm not convinced!

"Here—I'm 'me.' Everyone knows Falik, and Falik knows everyone. Here I have my own house. Yes, with an old, torn roof, but it's my own. I have a place here, and even after I pass away, whoever will happen to go by my grave in the local cemetery, will know that here lies Falik the Tailor. I was born in this town, lived and earned an honest living here, and nobody will have anything bad to say about me, God forbid.

"But what will I be there in America? A dried-up leaf torn from a tree, carried by a wind to a foreign woodland far away, surrounded by trees with younger and greener leaves.

"Who will I be there? What will belong to me? While alive— a stranger, a vagabond. And when dead—alone and forgotten. As time passes, the wind will bury my grave in sand, and no one will know that once there lived a Falik, and that very same Falik has died."

"But our children are there," Matle replied. "We'll belong to them there. The same as they belong to us."

"God only knows," sighed Falik. "Something tells me that they'll suddenly want us to start a new life there, to become young all over again. It will be hard for us to get used to that. And as time passes and they see that we can't become young again and live the way they live, we'll only be in their way and never hear a kind word from them again as we read now in their letters.

"No, Matle, it's a lot easier for them to write, 'Come here,' than for us to actually make the journey."

"So don't go," Matle said. "No one's forcing you."

"That's also easier said than done," Falik replied. "Can you convince yourself to never see your own children again before

you die? Never see their brides or their children? And die knowing that your children, whom you delivered in pain, carried
next to your heart, brought up with great worry and toil, will
never see your grave? And who knows whether they'll remember to say Kaddish for you or even light a memorial candle?"

Matle couldn't hold back her tears.

"We may cry and moan because of the evil decree that is
America!" said Falik, expressing his compassion for Matle and
what was in his own unhappy heart.

"Our parents knew nothing of America and didn't suffer our
sorrows. Ever since Jews began sailing for America, the parents
have become chickens, and the children—ducks! We stand at
the edge of the water and watch with dread as our children swim
across the ocean. We can't swim after them. We remain on the
shore and long to see them again, but with very little hope.

"No, Matle, no. Say what you will, our parents did not know
this kind of torture and suffering!" Falik banged his hand on
the table and began reciting the afternoon prayers.

So he sat in his shop, stabbing the needle into the fabric
like a machine. His thoughts tossed him every which way, as
in a fever. Suddenly it was all settled: He would remain and
die here beneath his own roof, where he had spent so many
years. And then a thought came to him, and he asked himself,
"What kind of father am I? What won't parents do for their
children? Did our forefather Jacob not leave his dear land
Canaan in his elder years and go forth to Egypt for the sake of
his son Joseph? 'The sons inherit the deeds of the forefathers.'
Maybe with this, the Torah is really teaching us that we have
no choice but to do the same: Leave our birthplace, our own

house, the synagogue, and everything we hold dear in this town, and set out far across the sea to America because our children are there and call us to them? If that's the way you want it, Almighty God, so be it."

At night, however, when he lay in bed and weighed everything that he had mulled over all day long, he suddenly asked himself, "How can I compare myself with our forefather Jacob? God said to him, 'Go,' so he went! But how do I know that God commands me to go?

"I only know that within me the Evil Inclination is at war with the Good Inclination. One says, 'Falik, don't budge from where you are! Don't sell your house. Don't travel to America. You'll regret it, but it'll be too late!'

"And the other says, 'Parents must follow their children! Thousands of Jews go to America, and God Himself probably shows them the way. Don't think you're smarter than the whole world. You, too, should go where everyone is going! Be a father to your children, remind them about God, and live to take pride in them in America.'

"It seems to me that both arguments have merit, but it's clear that the Good Inclination presents one, and the Evil Inclination presents the other. So be clever and figure out which one is the Good and which one is the Evil Inclination."

Chapter Twelve

THE WORRY ABOUT the roof let Falik be for a few days. Not because the weather was good and he thought it would stay that way all winter, but because his head was completely occupied with the worry about whether to go to the children—or not.

It struck him that it was precisely for this reason that the weather was fine. Maybe he heard no complaints from his tenants about being rained on so he could come to a decision—here or there—with a clear head.

But apparently, when the period that God had given him to think it over had passed, along came a storm that did enormous damage, not only to his roof but to more respectable roofs as well.

"Aha," said Falik to his Matle, listening to the wind rip through the roof. "The Old Man is in a rage now, probably angry because the foolish human is taking too much time to think. What do you say, Matle? Should I go over to Shaya's to tell him that I'm selling him my house in order to emigrate to America? Or do we decide once and for all to remain here, and trust in God's mercy that He will surely send help so that we can at least get through the winter in our own house?"

"It's better not to ask me," Matle answered. "A mother's heart is not the same as a father's. The children are dearer to me than ten such houses, especially since Toybele, her husband, and the little children—may they be well—are planning to leave for America after Passover."

"Does this mean you're saying I should sell the house?" Falik asked, desiring a more explicit answer.

"I'm not making any suggestions! Follow your heart, Husband, and whatever you do should be God's will," she replied.

Falik actually wished his wife would express her own opinion clearly so he could latch on to something and the decision to sell or not sell wouldn't get so jumbled up in his thoughts—one minute here, the next minute there. But Matle threw the whole burden on him. On his own, he had no idea how to best resolve the situation.

By nightfall, the wind had died down.

"You see, Matle," Falik said to his wife at bedtime, "the stronger the wind, the sooner it blows over. A person should never despair, I tell you, even when a storm like that rushes through his thoughts. I know that it was a wise man who once said, 'This too shall pass.'"

Falik recited the prayers, thanked God that there was no rain, and lay down to sleep. His head, exhausted from so many straight days of hard thinking, immediately sank into a deep sleep.

How long he slept undisturbed like that, he couldn't tell, but something suddenly awakened him. He opened his eyes. It was completely dark. However, he could hear pounding and murmuring.

Was it the sound of carts driving through the street? Were the firemen hurrying somewhere?

No! He thought the noise came from above—perhaps rain or hail drumming on the roof? No, a solid stream seemed to be pouring down, and before he was even fully awake, he suddenly felt a shower of water falling onto the quilt. It soon splashed in one spot and then another, and after the splashes, he heard a series of drips.

"Falik, get up! We're being flooded!" Matle cried out from her bed. And before he had a chance to stand up, he heard violent banging on the door, a great clamor, and his tenants' voices, "Our dear landlord sleeps like a count! For any rent money we give him, may God give him heartache."

Falik crawled out of bed. There was already a river on the floor, and wherever he turned, drops of water fell on his head, on his shoulders, and all over him. With trembling hands, he managed to strike a match and light the lamp.

A disaster, an evil decree. It poured down from all sides.

"Are you opening up or not?" shouted the tenants. "We're going to break down your door!"

Falik ran, lamp in hand, and opened the door. The tenants pushed their way in, yelling, "Come, see what's happening in your beloved apartments. The blood of our enemies should flow the way it's poured on us and all our belongings."

Falik remembered that on his worktable lay merchandise a customer had brought the night before. On his wall hung clothes that didn't belong to him, and he ran to rescue them so they wouldn't get wet.

A tenant grabbed him by the sleeve and shouted, "I won't let go! At least come and see for yourself how my bedclothes have been ruined. You will pay for the damage in court!"

"The same for me!" cried another tenant.

"And us, too!" shouted the rest without loosening their hold.

"Bandits, let me at least rescue the clothing and fabric that aren't mine!" Falik begged, and threw himself at the table.

Matle stood by her husband and also suffered curses and abuse at the hands of the tenants.

"If you're poor and can't afford to fix your roof, you shouldn't have a house either!" one tenant screamed.

"Not having enough money is one thing, but he has it and doesn't want to spend it! Tenants who pay rent, aren't they people too?" another one shouted.

"Even a pigsty in a decent house would be better than his apartments!" cried the widow living in the kitchen.

"What a calamity! I'm completely drenched. I'm trembling, I'm so wet and cold!"

"Cover the child with your jacket," cried a young wife to her husband. "He'll catch a chill and come down with croup, God forbid, from this wonderful apartment!"

The tenant covered the child with his jacket as he also shivered from the cold.

"Come, people! We're better off on the street," someone joked. "At least there we'll have clean water pouring down on us. Here it's clay and lime."

Falik heard it all, and his heart stopped. He was getting dripped on, too, but didn't feel it. Even worse, it felt as if his own blood was pouring out.

It rained like that for a full hour, nonstop. Falik thought he'd never live to see another day. Finally on the street, the rain stopped altogether. In the house, the drops were also less frequent. But no one even considered going back to bed. The bedclothes were soaking wet. In the bedrooms, the mud was knee-high.

As best they could, Falik and Matle helped the tenants wash the mud out of their rooms and hang out their things to dry. After that, they began to clean up for themselves. Neither of them could speak. Both were too disheartened, too numb.

By daybreak, the sky had cleared, and a bright warm sun appeared. "You see, Falik," Matle tried to cheer up her crestfallen husband, "God is not lacking in pity. With one hand He beats you, and with the other, He heals. We'll be able to drag everything out to the courtyard to dry in the sun."

As if his tongue had been snatched away, Falik didn't respond. Once he had finished his morning prayers and Matle began taking things out of the cupboard for his breakfast, Falik said, "How can anyone think about food now? Give me my walking stick. I'm going across to Shaya to sell him the house."

Matle trembled. The bread she was about to place on the table fell from her hand, and tears came to her eyes.

"Why are you crying, fool?" Falik tried to console her and didn't realize that his eyes were filling with tears too. "After all, you can see that God Himself drives us from our house without pity! He must need our bones for an American cemetery someplace. It's hard to battle Him with ordinary human strength."

Matle was in despair and couldn't reply.

"Don't cry, I beg you!" he implored his loyal wife, his own voice soaked with tears. "Don't let me lose my resolve! I'll go to Shaya the way I'd go to a doctor who has to cut out a piece of my heart."

"It must be that God wants us to enjoy our children in America with our own eyes," Matle consoled herself and her husband. Falik kissed the mezuzah on the doorpost and left.

As it happened, he found Shaya at home, but occupied with a landowner. Shaya's wife asked Falik to wait a minute until her husband was available to speak to him.

Falik took a seat.

Shaya's wife began to interrogate him about why he had come to see her husband, but Falik would not and could not answer her. Now he hated her seven times more than before.

"Why are you afraid to tell me?" she pestered him. "As I see it, your concerns are my concerns. There are no secrets from a wife."

"Have a little patience," Falik replied, trying to get rid of her. "You'll find out soon enough."

"Maybe you need an interest-free loan?" she asked. "Right now my husband himself is looking for a loan. Just today, he has to go with the landowner to pick up his wheat. I don't know if you've ever in your life seen as much money as he handed over to that landowner just a moment ago!"

Falik couldn't help thinking, "If only Shaya would say that he no longer has the money to buy my house."

"Anyway, if you want to try to take out a loan, it's no sin, but you'll just have to sit here and wait. It may take a while," she said, hoping to be rid of him, in case he really did want an interest-free loan.

"Won't he be going out soon?" asked Falik, starting to regret the whole business. But just as he reached the door to leave,
Shaya came out of the office. Seeing Falik, he said to him
warmly, "Good morning, Reb Falik! No doubt you've come on
account of what we've discussed? Very good of you! Now I see
that you are a man of your word."

"What can you do," answered Falik, "when the children
want you to join them in America, and God Himself urges you
on as if with a whip? And when you have no choice, you say
to yourself, 'Almighty God, if this is what you want, so be it!' "

"You're doing the right thing, Reb Falik. Very smart! You
have nothing to lose. The Jewish situation here becomes more
restrictive and bitter every day. Our livelihoods suffer, there's
hatred and jealousy on all sides. While there is still time, whoever hurries over there before America is completely flooded with
our little Jews, is fortunate. There, you can still succeed at anything you want. Later, I'm afraid it won't be any better than it
is here. If only I had children in America who would send for
me, I would sell everything, lock, stock, and barrel this very
day, spit on all my success in this country, and hasten to
America."

"And in the meantime," thought Falik to himself, "he
builds himself a house—a palace! He converts his mill into an
oil press, and if that isn't enough, he wants to swallow up my
poor house, too."

Shaya said, "It's a shame I now have to go with the landowner to pick up his wheat. Otherwise I would conclude our
business one, two, three. But tomorrow, or at the latest the day
after tomorrow, I'll return, with God's help. I'll send for you,

Reb Falik. I beg you, have patience for a few days. I won't go back on my word, and if you want, we can shake on it while we're standing here."

"There's no rush, Reb Shaya! Two or three days is no big deal. I won't speak to anyone else. Good day, Reb Shaya!" Falik blurted out and quickly slipped out the door.

Once out on the street, Falik breathed a sigh of relief. "Thank God. Thank God! Saved by a hair. I was almost no longer a householder, no longer Falik! Now, however, I return to my house, to my own home. Don't punish me, dear God. I have never felt so strongly about how dear and beloved my house is to me!"

CHAPTER THIRTEEN

DURING THOSE FEW days that Shaya was at the landowner's estate, Falik did everything he could to avoid selling his house.

He met with a few householders of his acquaintance and tried to borrow fifty rubles or so in order to redo half the roof and repair the other half as best he could. He was willing to sign a promissory note, vowing not to enjoy even a bite of bread in his mouth until he'd paid back the fifty rubles with the utmost gratitude. But everyone came back with the same answer, "Who has rubles in ready money these days? We thank God when we're able to borrow a ruble ourselves from time to time when we have no choice and are at the end of our rope!"

People might not have been so cruel, and the town's free loan society might have guaranteed the fifty rubles, but the tenants had spread the word that Falik was selling his house and intended to join his sons in America. And with that, no one was willing to take the risk.

His son-in-law made matters even worse. Wherever he knew his father-in-law planned to ask for a loan, he declared beforehand that it would be very wrong to lend Falik even a kopek.

It was already well known that Shaya Miller had offered fifteen hundred rubles for the house, and he, Falik, had dug in his heels, "No, and no!" So instead of helping him out in his time of need, everyone tried to persuade him, "Just sell the house! Take the money. Help your son-in-law while you're at it and travel in good health to America."

Falik understood that his devoted son-in-law had a hand in this, and it was no longer worth his effort to try to obtain a respectable loan. His only option was to speak to Benzion the Loan Shark.

Benzion the Loan Shark himself had once proposed that Falik take a few rubles to be paid back in installments with interest. Falik, however, trembled at the thought of a loan from Benzion the way one reacts to the prospect of a fire. He knew that no poor property owner who had ever fallen into Benzion's clutches emerged unscathed.

"Your house, Reb Falik, needs a new roof," Benzion had said out of the blue last year after running into Falik in front of his door.

Not suspecting anything, Falik had answered him candidly at the time, "If I had the means to replace the roof, I would certainly spend it!"

"What do you mean 'you don't have it?'" asked Benzion. "You can have as much as I think your house is worth! Anyone with this kind of collateral doesn't have to worry about a thing. Just tell me how much you need, and I'll get the money together in cash. Today even."

In those days, the roof wasn't that badly damaged, and the need wasn't as pressing as it was now. Therefore, Falik thanked

Benzion for his kind heart and had a good laugh at his expense.

"He won't capture me with his sack!" Falik told himself at the time. "May God protect me from such compassionate people!"

Today, however, when he felt as if he was drowning and no one would reach out a hand to rescue him, Falik decided to try his last chance for help. He set off to find Benzion to grab onto the edge of the sword.

"How much would you like to borrow, Reb Falik?" Benzion asked.

"Do you think I know?" answered Falik. "I haven't the slightest idea how much a whole new roof costs. But the less I owe, the better for me, Reb Benzion. I think a hundred will do nicely."

The loan shark replied, "You're making a big mistake, Reb Falik. A house is a thief. As soon as you start making repairs, it becomes clear that you need this, you need that, and these days, with wood and labor as costly as gold, you might not even have enough for challah to make the blessing over bread.

"And while you're at it, why not fix up the whole house? It's time for a little sprucing up, Reb Falik. Maybe replace the fence? With one thing and another, my guess is you need a good three hundred rubles at least. A little outside, a little inside, and before you know it, you'll have spent the whole three hundred.

"But as a result," the loan shark reassured him, "your house will hold its own against respectable houses. And you know the old saying, 'If it's worth doing at all, it's worth doing well!' You, Reb Falik, are no barefoot peasant. You know, of course, what comes from patching and pasting."

"You are right, Reb Benzion," Falik replied. "My house needs a lot of work, but not for three hundred rubles like you say. Let's shake on it. A hundred and fifty is also too much. I don't want to borrow more than a hundred, and I don't dare."

"Why not? What are you afraid of?"

"Don't forget that these are hard times in the world, and I'm not making much," answered Falik. "Let's hope I can repay the hundred in a year's time. That's all I ask from the Almighty."

"Take at least two hundred rubles, Reb Falik. That's my advice!"

"Why do you want this so badly, Reb Benzion?" inquired Falik, suspicious of the lender's motives.

"For your benefit, Reb Falik! I wouldn't want you to come to a standstill halfway through. By the way, of course, I want the renovations to be tasteful!"

"What's the difference to you whether they're tasteful or not?"

"Does it have to be spelled out?" Benzion asked. "If your house looks presentable, I and my investment are more secure. Don't you see?"

"No!" Falik said firmly. "Don't talk me into it. I must not. I'm not interested! You and your investment are certainly safe, unless I don't survive of course! You will get back your hundred, plus interest, and with the greatest thanks, Reb Benzion!"

"All right, let it be as you say," the lender finally gave in. "Bring me the deed to your house, if you have it. If not, let's go to the notary and write up a contract, just as it should be, properly signed and sealed. And, as a matter of fact, you'll take the hundred right there in front of him and hand me the document that we'll prepare!

"And don't forget to take the insurance policy from the safe," the loan shark remembered to add. "Without the policy, your house isn't worth a single copper coin to me."

"Good," answered Falik. "I'll head home and bring you everything you ask for, Reb Benzion." But in his heart, Falik thought, "Humiliate me as much as you want, loan shark and bloodsucker. You won't trap me in your net!"

Back home, he said to Matle, "There are all kinds of creatures in God's world. You want a Shaya? Here's a Shaya with the appetite of a hungry wolf that wants to swallow up the whole world. You want a distinguished scholar who invokes God at every turn, who claims only to do favors for others, I give you Reb Benzion the Lender. May God, blessed be He, protect us from his favors and advice!"

"What does he want from you?" Matle asked.

"Only that I sign a paper offering the house as collateral for the hundred rubles that I want to borrow. And in the meantime, he already wants me to bring him the insurance policy from the safe. And, do you know what his intention is, Matle? His intention is to inherit from us while we're still alive. He'll probably make out the document to tie me up hand and foot so that no good Jew will be able to untie me."

"Anything in the world, Husband," said Matle, "but don't have anything to do with this loan shark and bloodsucker!"

"But what should I do?" moaned Falik, as if sick, and his misery forced a groan out of him. "You can see that the Creator of the Universe has blocked all roads and left us with only one way out: Decide between Shaya Miller and Benzion the Loan Shark. It's very clear. Either sell or lose the house, God forbid."

"Of course it's more sensible to sell!" said Matle. "Let there be an end to it! Do you hear, Husband? Let there be an end, I tell you. I see you suffering. Your face is black as the earth. God in Heaven, the world isn't coming to an end. Is it worth it to give up your life over these four old walls?"

"Not worth it, you say?" asked Falik.

"Your health is more important to me!"

"Are you saying: 'Sell?'"

"It's God's will, Husband! A person's will has as much influence as a stalk of burnt straw."

"Good! I'll wait until Shaya comes back."

"Do you have any other choice?" asked Matle.

"A choice? Benzion? I don't know. Maybe I'll take someone with experience when we draw up the contract so that Benzion won't choke me with his hundred rubles."

"Don't even consider Benzion, Falik," Matle said firmly. "Shaya is no saint, maybe not even a good man. But Shaya is willing to buy and pay up. Benzion, on the other hand, is pious, but he'll even fleece the angels. He doesn't want to purchase, but only to swindle. Benzion is a leech, a bloodsucker. Run from him, Husband!"

"Good, good! You have spoken. I will act on it," Falik agreed.

Chapter Fourteen

A FEW DAYS passed after that conversation with his wife, and Falik made a firm decision: He would sell the house to Shaya.

"It's God's will. It's hopeless. There's nothing you can do, Falik," he told himself. He waited nervously for Shaya, the way a sick man waits in torture for the doctor to come and perform a difficult operation.

However, he didn't hear from Shaya. Several days passed, and Shaya had still not sent for him as he had promised.

Falik didn't even know whether Shaya had returned from the landowner's. It would have been very easy for him to find out. All he had to do was leave his house, go over to Shaya's building, and inquire of Shaya's people who were supervising the workmen already covering the roof. But somehow, he did not want to ask, as if afraid to mention Shaya's name to a stranger.

And the sky cleared up. The sun was radiant and warm, and it was as if there was no such thing as autumn in God's world. It was possible to believe that a house with a leaky roof didn't have to dread wind or rain, the way Falik's heart always did.

Jumbled thoughts filled Falik's head. "Maybe Shaya took sick at the landowner's? Maybe bandits armed with guns ran out from the forest and attacked and murdered him, or took his last groschen? Now buying a house would be out of the question. Or maybe Shaya doesn't want to buy the house anymore. What does he need it for? Doesn't he have enough houses?"

And all the while, the sun shone as if in the middle of summer with no wind and no clouds. The old shingles lay quiet and calm on Falik's roof, and they seemed to speak to him, "What do you have against us? For forty years you've lived beneath us. For forty years we've endured all the gales and downpours and never let a drop of rain fall on you. Now, in the forty-first year, now that we're old and weak and lack the strength to protect you and your tenants from the rain from time to time, you're angry with us, and you want to get rid of us and your house altogether! What have you against your house?"

And Falik raised his head towards the sky and saw how clear, high, blue, and infinite it was.

"Creator of the Universe," his heart spoke to God, "would it be so terrible if it was always like this? The sky always clear without clouds or rain? No, the world needs rain, but it should rain on the fields, on gardens, but not in the towns, or at least not on the houses whose owners can't figure out how to repair their leaky roofs!"

And when night fell and Falik saw the starry sky, he praised and thanked God for His mercy that he could fall asleep. But the fear that he might, God forbid, experience another night like the one just last week, made his life bitter.

In the meantime, the days passed one after another, and there were times when Falik managed to convince himself that maybe his ordeal would end. Maybe he would get by without Shaya. Winter was about to set in with its dry frost, and even if there was snow, that was a lot better than rain. Some solution could be found for snow, even melted snow.

And early one morning, when the sun was, indeed, radiant and warm and Falik's window stood open, he was for some reason feeling in such a good mood that he almost forgot about Shaya and all of his worries altogether.

Matle had just set the table and put out the bread and salt cellar. She told Falik it was time to wash his hands and say the blessing and went back into the kitchen to dish out what she had cooked for breakfast.

Falik washed his hands, said the prayer, dipped a piece of bread into the salt, and recited the blessing. Before he had even taken a piece of bread into his mouth, the door opened, and in walked some young stranger, who said, "The boss has asked if Reb Falik would be so kind as to go see him tonight at six."

Falik thought, "A customer must want me to measure him or do some other bit of work."

"Who is your employer?" he asked, pleased.

"Reb Shaya Miller," the boy answered and quickly left.

The food dropped out of Falik's mouth. His hands began to shake, and his face became as white as chalk.

Coming in with the bowl in her hands and seeing her husband so pale and trembling, Matle asked in alarm, "Husband, why are you so frightened? What is it? Who was here?"

"It's nothing, Matle," Falik said, wanting to reassure his wife, who stood there white and shaking, just looking at him.

"Then why are you so pale with your teeth chattering?"

"I don't feel well."

"Do you want some cold water?"

"No, no need."

"Maybe it's the fumes from the kitchen. Is your stomach upset? Let me see your tongue!"

"It's nothing. Nothing! It'll pass. But I think I'll eat later." He tried to pull himself together so as not to worry her.

"Is it your heart?" she asked, taking his hand. "Your hand—so cold and lifeless. Dear me! What happened to you? Maybe swallow a little brandy, revive your heart?"

"No, I don't need anything! Let me sit quietly."

"You're better off outside in the fresh air. The sun is shining. It's warm and bright in the courtyard. It's beautiful out."

And without waiting for him to consent, she took him by the hand as if he was an invalid and led him out of the house to a grassy slope in the courtyard facing the sun. They sat down together.

At first, Falik didn't say a word, didn't think about a thing, and just remained with a blank mind like someone in a faint. Matle warmed his hands and didn't take her eyes off him. Only then did he begin to revive and take in every little thing in the courtyard.

It seemed that his eyes wanted to say farewell to all that was before him at that moment. They darted about as if afraid they were seeing everything for the very last time. And all that he laid his eyes on now reminded him of events in his life, both glad and sad.

"Why do you look so unhappy, Falik?" asked his devoted wife.

"Take a look, Matle," he indicated with his hand. "Over there under the eaves, next to the attic window, I can still see the nails I hammered in with my own hand when we were both young, and you were about to deliver our first child."

He thought for a bit, then suddenly asked, "Do you remember why I put those nails in there?"

"Who can remember something that far back?"

"You wanted to dry apples. I bought a whole box of juicy apples. You sliced them, threaded them on a long string, and said to me, 'Falik, where can we hang these in the sun so they'll dry out?' I didn't have to think for too long, grabbed the tall ladder with the help of two of the workmen, crawled up myself, hammered in the nails myself, and hung the strings of apples. And all winter long you cooked me a sweet applesauce on Friday night. Don't you remember?"

"Do I remember?"

"And those hooks in the fence, where you used to run a rope to hang the wash! Do you remember?

"So what if I remember?" she asked, having no idea why he was reminding her about such trifles.

"And do you remember this, Matle, how thirty-something years ago, we sat on this slope, just like now, on a Shabbes afternoon? Our oldest rolled around on the grass, and our hearts were full of happiness and joy. 'See, Matle,' I said to you then, 'am I not a king? Are you not my beautiful queen? And our pretty child, is he not a fortunate prince? And everything we see now, isn't this our kingdom? See, Matle,' I said, 'the ground beneath us, the grass, the house, the fence, the well, even the blue sky over our heads, are ours, Matle, ours. We didn't take any of it away from anyone by force, we didn't inherit it from my father, but I earned it all with my own two hands and honest toil. Am I not the luckiest man in the world?'

"I don't recall what you answered at that time," Falik continued, suddenly animated, "but I remember your beautiful eyes, Matle, with which you looked at me then, and I felt even richer and happier at that moment."

"Who cares?" she said with a heartfelt sigh. "What happened then is in the past. But what about now?"

"Today, too, Matle, I'm lucky and rich because I've never forgotten any of it. When I think back, it seems that time hasn't gone by at all, and I feel the same joy in my heart as long ago. And do you know what, Matle?" said Falik, holding her hand in his. "Do you know how pretty you were and how much I loved you? I wouldn't have traded one glance from you or one kiss from your sweet lips for a princess!"

"Old man, do you still have such silly notions? How is it you aren't ashamed to talk such nonsense, you with your white beard?"

"Nonsense, you say?" he replied. "But what's the sense in living if not for that kind of nonsense? Matle, what appeal would old age have if people couldn't sometimes recall the happiness and pleasure of their younger years? What you call 'nonsense.' Without that nonsense, we would never have been young and never have grown old!"

Matle let out a sigh as if to say, "Really, is it worth it to reach old age if you have so much suffering and worry?"

"And imagine, Matle, if someone were to come to us, sitting here so old and weak, and say, 'Listen, Falik, I'm leaving a million rubles in cash here for you. Give up your gloomy old wife, Matle.' What should I reply to such a proposal?"

"Who in their right mind would give you even a groschen for me today? All you get from me now are trials and tribulations!"

"Maybe a lunatic. Maybe someone sane. I'm just giving you an example!"

"Do I know what you're going on about? I don't have any idea what you want from me."

"I want to know whether it would be proper for me to sell you to that person, whether crazy or sane, for money, because now you are old, and all I get from you is grief, as you yourself say?"

"No, it would not be right, Husband!"

"Why not?" Falik asked.

"Because one mustn't part from someone with whom one has been content in their younger years, even though all you have is woes and worries in your later years!"

"Good that you understand!" observed Falik. "Today, tell me, my own dear Matle, why do you ask me, with such a light heart, to sell our house, because it's now old and gloomy, and all we get from it is headaches and hardships? Where is your sense of justice, Matle?"

"How can you compare a house to a wife?" she asked.

"How? Just listen, Matle, to what I will tell you. The preacher at our small tailors' synagogue once said in a sermon that one of our holy rabbinic sages always called his wife, 'My house.' And do you know why?

"Why?"

"The preacher explained it. Because just as God grants man a wife, He also grants him a house and home. And therefore, our preacher said, we Jews call a young man 'Little Master of the House' after his wedding. This is the explanation: That young man is no longer a fancy-free creature without any foundation, someone who's here today and takes off to the mountains tomorrow. And it's all because he now has a wife, a mistress of the house, may she live to be one hundred and twenty.

"And so, only for this reason, Matle, we see in the world that when a man loves his wife, he also loves his house and his home. He cherishes and loves his house and home because he cherishes and loves his wife, the mistress of his house. God forbid, on the contrary: If his wife is not dear to him, his house is not a well-loved home either but a dark prison from which he wants to tear himself away and run off if he possibly can.

"And now that you understand, Shaya can send his hosts of servants after me, he can chase me himself, he can offer everything he owns for me to sell him the house, but I am not Falik your husband if I even give him the time of day!

"And now that you understand me, Matle, and I've taken an oath, let there be thunder and lightning, rain or hail—it's not my worry! Never mind. Just because a head lacks a hat, no one sells his head! As long as there's a head, we'll find a hat for it!

"Now come inside and let me eat. I feel like a new man."

With these words, Falik picked himself up in the best of spirits and went inside on his own with no help from Matle.

She was barely able to keep up.

Chapter Fifteen

THREE WEEKS AFTER that conversation with his wife, Falik sat in his shop with his sleeves rolled up and wrote this little letter to his children in America:

> To my dear and beloved children, you should live and be well, amen!
>
> First of all, I write to you that I and your dear mother, Matle, my own wife, long may she live, are, thank God, healthy. May God let us hear the same from you always, but with fewer troubles!
>
> Second of all, I write to you that God, blessed be He, who has always helped me succeed in my small way, without help from the children, has to-day also sent his good messenger, who has helped me in my moment of greatest need, without any favors from you.
>
> My house already has, thanks be to God, a new roof!
>
> Not even shingles or tin, but a roof made of fine new boards. Let's hope that God sends us as many

years living in our own house as the roof will remain intact and good for us!

The good messenger, whom God sent me, is Kasriel the Lumber Merchant!

I was absolutely miserable, walking around in the street, worrying, "What am I going to do? How will I find a solution?" Kasriel came up to me, completely out of the blue. He had been away all summer, and I had never thought to have any dealings with him before.

He's an important merchant with forestry and lumber interests. What have I got to do with him? But if the Almighty God wants to help someone, your worries don't matter.

"Reb Falik," he said to me in the street, just like that, pointing to my roof. "As I see it, your house desperately needs a new roof, and I understand why you don't actually get around to replacing it.

"It's simple. You lack the few rubles you need to get it done. Am I right?

"Hear what I have to tell you: I have need of a courtyard where I can keep my boards and other lumber. Lease me half your courtyard for three years to store my lumber, and I'll fix you up with a new roof. Even better, as a matter of fact, I'll do a little work on the house itself, repair the fence, and put in a new gate. In short, Reb Falik, I'll turn you into a real householder!"

So, children, what do you say? Was this not an angel from heaven sent by God Himself to relieve me of my suffering and worries? Say what you want, children, but God punished me only because, for one moment, I hoped for help from you and not from Him. I thank Him for His punishment, the same as for His help! From now on, I'll know what someone can hope for when it comes to getting help from the children.

You wrote that you wouldn't send any money because you want me to come stay with you no matter what. You are afraid to send me the few rubles in case I might spend it on a new roof for my "old shack," as you call your once beloved home where you first set eyes on God's world, because then I wouldn't want to come over to you in America.

I believe you, dear children. This is very nice and very fine of you! But it would have been ten times nicer and finer had you actually sent the rubles and written in your note, "Papa, you ask for a few rubles to put on a roof for our old home. We happily send you the money with our good wishes, but we beg you, don't let this prevent you and Mama from coming to visit us in America!"

Now, however, my own dear children, since you did not have enough good sense and decency, and explicitly wrote that you are not sending me money to put a roof on the house so that your mother and I will have to come to you, in good health, I must tell you this: One mustn't pressure anyone. Not a daughter of Israel, not a son of Israel, and not even your own father.

No, good and devoted children, what's true is true. You are good and devoted, but you could also be wiser and more gracious. Your letter wasn't very smart, and if that is considered smart and good in America, then I would prefer to die a fool here where I was born!

As for coming to you, as you ask and wish, I'd like to write a few words here. Just use your brains and good sense so that you understand my words correctly.

For me to tell you that we don't want to travel to you at all would not be true. How could a father not want to be close to his children and see them at least once a day? Or even to go over and take a look at what you're doing there in America and see the life you have made for yourselves that you always write about in your letters? To actually see your brides, if God wishes it, talk to them, and know at least who and what my daughters-in-law will be?

And why deny it? I'm as sinful as anybody else, and as it happens, a sinful person also sometimes desires, as long as his eyes are still open, to wander away from his birthplace and take a good look at God's little world. His heart yearns to see what he's not yet seen. For example, magnificent cities and beautiful buildings, houses, and palaces that people who travel describe.

Certainly there is much to see and marvel at: mountains, lakes, great rivers, and wide seas with boats and ships that sail on them. Not to die a fool who doesn't know what to answer should they ask me when I come to the Next World, "So, tell us, Falik, what have you seen in God's great world other than the small town where you were born?"

I can imagine the laughter when someone like that answers, "I've seen my little town, my synagogue, my bathhouse, and my bathhouse attendant. Seen the Jews and non-Jews of my acquaintance, all the town's goats, hens, and roosters, and nothing more."

"Fool," they would have to shout up there. "For what purpose did God give you eyes and create hands and feet that you didn't have the sense to see the world properly?"

You see, I understand it, children. I understand it very well and would very much like to see something too. Obviously you'll ask, "Since it is so, Papa, isn't it even a greater wrong that you don't want to come visit us?"

You're right, my children, but I'm not completely wrong. Just listen to what I tell you. Coming to you, remaining there to live out the rest of my years near you, is something that simply can't happen. You'll ask, "Why not?" and I will answer you. Children, a young sapling is easily ripped out and can be replanted somewhere else, even as far away as America. It soon takes to the new soil, roots, thrives, and flourishes. An old tree, children, doesn't let anyone rip it out unless you chop it down or break it into pieces. Plant it somewhere else in foreign soil, and it won't grow anymore and will, in fact, dry out and rot. Why fool yourselves, children? Your mother and I are now old trees.

Don't badger us. Don't search for new soil where you can replant us. If you want us to continue to live on this earth, leave us in the place where we were planted right from the start and where we've already grown and flourished during our lives.

Again, as for traveling to see you for a visit to enjoy a few weeks with you and then to return home, that, I admit, would be in order. But even better, children, would be if you took the same trip to visit us, and not we to you. And do you know why? Simple: your new home, America, will never run away from you. When you want to return, you'll find the same America. But for us, God forbid, it could be disastrous not to find a new home and to lose the old one.

Children, make your way here sometime. See how your father's house has become whole and new again. See how your father and your mother live, thank God, may He be blessed, once more happy and content under their own roof where they feel the whole world is theirs and they're as rich as can be.

Come, children, take pleasure in seeing
me, your father, Falik Sherman, and me,
your mother, who greets you in turn, and

who invites you, of course, to come, so
that we'll all see each other in good health,
Matle Sherman

And indeed, Falik wrote the truth to his children. Now he
really does feel that the whole world is his and he is as rich as
anyone. He is pleased with his house, with the new roof, and
with Kasriel the Lumber Merchant, who is nothing but a good
tenant who keeps the courtyard clean and tidy as it should be.

Matle is certainly delighted. In the warehouse in the courtyard, there are always wood chips, small boards, and other kinds
of wood that come in handy for a housewife in the kitchen.
Kasriel's people in the warehouse hold the mistress of the
house in high esteem and take it upon themselves to select the
best and driest chips for her. And indeed, the same people who
work for Kasriel also rent the rooms formerly occupied by those
poor tenants who caused Falik so much suffering. Now Falik has
better tenants and worries less about the insurance and tax
money, which also arrives with less difficulty. He has every
right to be content.

But on one point, Falik is not satisfied, and that is the
neighbor across the way, Shaya Miller. And every time he has
to thread a needle in the afternoon, he repeats with anger, "This
is what the poor homeowner gets from the wealthy neighbor
who lives opposite him! He blocked half my light, that Shaya,
and cut off a big chunk of my day. For everyone else, it's still
broad daylight. Here in this room, however, it's already dark."

And when he says that, he rises from his workbench, goes
over to the window, gives his eyes a good rub, and aims the tip
of the thread at the eye of the needle. He often has to poke his

head out the window and hold up the needle, just as if he's borrowing a bit of light from the street in order to see the tiny hole of the needle more clearly.

And yet, when he lifts up his head and his eyes catch sight of the house facing his, he looks at the fancy cornice and the two balconies on the second floor for a few minutes, and then says to himself, "I have complaints against Shaya, that rat, but against the house—none. Say what you will, the house is a beautiful house, after all. Cleverly constructed, simply a delight for the eye!"

Acknowledgments

Several people were kind enough to contribute their expertise through the wonders of email. Many thanks to Agnes Romer Segal in Calgary, Canada, and Aliza Krauz in Vienna, Austria, for helping with particularly tricky passages, and for giving me confidence. Rabbi Eli Rosenfeld and Mrs. Raizel Rosenfeld of Chabad Lubavitch of Portugal, and Miriam Swirsky, in Lisbon, explained Hebrew quotations. Thomas Soxberger in Vienna knew about yellow powder useful for nursing mothers. Eszter Langer in Dusseldorf helped with German words and phrases. Sheldon Londner in Los Angeles graciously gave me the invaluable *Verterbukh fun loshn-koydesh-shtamike verter in yidish* (*Dictionary of Words of Hebrew and Aramaic Origin in Yiddish*).

Thank you to the Yiddish Conversation Circle at the Soloway Jewish Community Center in Ottawa for inviting me to join their group on Zoom. Miri Koral of the California Institute for Yiddish Culture and Language has brought many wonderful Yiddish programs to the Los Angeles community for over twenty years. I credit her for prompting me to begin translating, and for introducing me to Jacob Dinezon.

Thank you to the following readers for checking the text so carefully: Arthur Clark, Robin Evans, Lynn Padgett, Carolyn Toben, and Mary Alice Wollam.

I am indebted to Scott Hilton Davis for the gift of *Falik un zayn hoyz*. He has been the perfect editor: wise, knowledgeable, patient, kind, and funny. I owe him much for turning this into so polished a book.

And to my family: My daughters Robin Stein for her thoughtful reading, and Natalie Stein for the dictionaries and support. And above all, my husband Robert Stein, who makes all things possible.

Mindy Liberman

ABOUT THE AUTHOR

JACOB DINEZON was born in New Zagare, Lithuania, in the early 1850s. His father died when he was twelve, and he was sent to live with an uncle in the Russian town of Mohilev.

An excellent student, Dinezon was hired by a wealthy family to tutor their young daughter. While living in their household, he became a trusted member of the family and was soon promoted to bookkeeper and manager of the family business. Through this family, Dinezon was introduced to the owner of a famous Jewish publishing company in Vilna called The Widow and Brothers Romm, which published his first novel, *The Dark Young Man*, in 1877. The book became a runaway bestseller.

Moving to Warsaw in the 1890s, Dinezon quickly became a prominent figure in the city's Jewish literary circle. He befriended almost every major Jewish writer of his day, including Sholem Abramovitsh (Mendele Mocher Sforim; 1835–1917), Sholem Aleichem (1859–1916), and I. L. Peretz (1852–1915). These writers are the classic writers of modern Yiddish literature, and Peretz became Dinezon's closest friend and confidant.

Over the next twenty years, Dinezon published several works of fiction, including *A Stumbling Block in the Road, Hershele: A Jewish Love Story, Yosele: A Story from Jewish Life, Falik and His House,* and *The Crisis: A Story of the Lives of Merchants.* He wrote sentimental novels about urban life in the Russian Empire and focused on the emotional conflicts affecting Jewish life as modern ideas challenged long-established religious practices and traditions. The plight of his characters often brought tears to the eyes of his devoted readers and remained in their memories long after they finished his stories.

During the First World War, Jacob Dinezon helped found an orphanage and schools to care for Jewish children made homeless by the fighting between Russia and Germany. He died in 1919 and is buried in Warsaw's Jewish cemetery beside I. L. Peretz.

About the Translator

MINDY LIBERMAN studied Yiddish at McGill University. She has translated poetry by Miriam Ulinover and letters by Sholem Aleichem. Her work has been published in *In geveb: A Journal of Yiddish Studies* and on the JacobDinezon.com website. She is a retired librarian living in Los Angeles.

Reading and Discussion Questions

1. In the first chapter, Jacob Dinezon establishes the deep connection Falik has with his house. He portrays the two as old friends who have aged together and gone from prosperity to hard times. How does this depiction of their relationship set the stage for the conflicts to follow? How does Dinezon introduce and develop the themes of home and homeownership, and how do these themes resonate with you?

2. Through the letters they write to each other, Falik and his adult children express conflicting views about repairing the old house. How do their opposing perspectives reflect the differences in their ages and life situations? If Falik and Matle were your parents, would you send them money to repair the run-down house where you grew up or try to persuade them to join you in America?

3. How does Dinezon depict the differences between the town's working poor and its wealthy residents? How does Falik the tailor's life differ from Shaya the miller's circumstances? Do we see similar class differences in today's society? How would you feel if a wealthy person bought the property across the street from your home, tore down the existing house, and built an extravagant mansion in its place?

4. Scenes of Falik's religious practices and deeply held faith are woven throughout the story. In his letters to his sons in America, he expresses his concerns about their changes in appearance and displays of prosperity. He fears their new lifestyle may lead them away from their religion. How do you think Falik's sons reacted to their father's words? How did Falik's steadfast religious and cultural attitudes influence his future decisions and actions?

5. We see that Falik loves and cares for his wife, Matle, but criticizes her intelligence and questions her ability to understand logic and reasoning. How did you respond to Falik's attitude? How did his views reflect the conditions, expectations, and constraints placed on women by the customs and practices of that time? How have women's lives changed since Dinezon wrote his novella? Are there still gender limitations and restrictions placed on individuals in modern communities?

6. To encourage Falik to sell his house, Shaya Miller says, "The Jewish situation here becomes more restrictive and bitter every day. Our livelihoods suffer, there's hatred and jealousy on all sides. . . . If only I had children in America who would send for me, I would sell everything, lock, stock, and barrel this very day, spit on all my success in this country, and hasten to America." What motivated Shaya to say this to Falik? Knowing what we know now, how does Shaya's statement foreshadow the devastating events that awaited the Jews of Russia and Eastern Europe who did not emigrate?

7. Sitting in the courtyard near the end of the story (pages 107–111), Falik shares his memories with Matle about their younger years and admits that his love for her is embodied in his de-

votion to their house. Falik tells Matle that when you love someone or something, you don't just discard it. "Just because a head lacks a hat," Falik says, "no one sells his head. As long as there's a head, we'll find a hat for it!" What was your reaction to this scene?

8. In the final chapter (pages 112–117), Falik writes to his sons in America to tell them of the miracle that has taken place to allow him to remain in his home: that through Divine intervention, Kasriel the Lumber Merchant arrived out of the blue to rescue him and his house. How was this ending supported by the way Falik's faith and religious life were portrayed through the story? How did you react to this ending?

9. Also, in the final chapter, Falik chastises his children for how they responded to his plea for help. He goes on to explain why he and their mother cannot move to live with them in America. He says, "An old tree, children, doesn't let anyone rip it out unless you chop it down or break it into pieces. Plant it somewhere else in foreign soil, and it won't grow anymore and will, in fact, dry out and rot. Why fool yourselves, children? Your mother and I are now old trees." How do you feel about this statement? Do you know older people who have had the energy and resilience to make a significant move and thrive? How would you fare in such a situation?

10. *Falik and His House* is set in the Russian Empire at the turn of the twentieth century. What lessons does it offer to us today about how to live in a changing world while holding on to our faith, identity, and values?

GLOSSARY

Aleinu. The closing prayer of all three daily prayer services. It was customary to spit once while reciting this prayer.

Challah. A braided, white bread eaten on the Sabbath and holidays.

Elul. The summer month in the Hebrew calendar used as a time of self-reflection and evaluation in preparation for the High Holidays.

Haggadah. The book of readings for the seder, a service including a ceremonial dinner held on the first or first and second evenings of Passover in commemoration of the exodus from Egypt.

High Holidays. The fall holidays of Rosh Hashanah and Yom Kippur.

Kaddish. An Aramaic prayer of praise to God. A version is recited by mourners in public services after the death of a close relative.

Kasriel. The Yiddish form of the name of the biblical angel Katriel, which means Crown of God.

Korach. The biblical figure who challenged Moses and Aaron's authority and was buried alive by God for his rebellion. Many stories are told of Korach's wealth.

L'chaim. A toast meaning "to life!"

Mezuzah. A box or case that contains a small parchment scroll with two blessings from the Torah. The mezuzah is fastened to the doorpost of a house or building.

Passover. A major spring holiday that commemorates the liberation of the Israelites from Egyptian slavery.

Pithom and Ramses. The two biblical cities the Pharaoh forced the Israelites to build for his treasury houses.

Reb. A term of respect used to address an adult male.

Rebbe. Teacher.

Rosh Hashanah. The Jewish New Year, observed in the fall.

Shabbes. The Sabbath.

Shabbes Bereishis. The first Sabbath after the High Holidays in the fall, when the first portion of Genesis is read in the synagogue.

Shabbes Nachamu. The Sabbath of Consolation following the fast of Tishah b'Av during the summer.

Shabbes Noah. The second Sabbath following the High Holidays in the fall, when the Genesis chapter about Noah is read in the synagogue.

Shavuos. A major Jewish festival held in the spring that celebrates the day God presented the Torah to the Jewish people at Mount Sinai.

Sukkah. A temporary hut or booth erected during the holiday of Sukkos.

Sukkos. An eight-day holiday celebrating the harvest and commemorating the escape from Egypt and the forty years spent dwelling in the desert.

Tannaim. The rabbinic sages whose teachings were recorded in the Mishnah in the first two centuries of the common era. The Mishna is the portion of the Talmud that contains the original version of the rabbinic oral laws.

Tefillin. Phylacteries. The leather boxes containing scrolls of parchment inscribed with verses from the Torah, which a Jewish man binds to his arm and forehead with leather straps during morning prayers.

Tishah b'Av. The Ninth of Av, observed during the summer. A fast day commemorating the destruction of the First and Second Temples in Jerusalem.

Torah. The holy scroll on which is written the five books of Moses.

Tzitzit. Fringes or tassels attached to prayer shawls and other garments as a reminder of biblical commandments.

Yom Kippur. The Day of Atonement, observed with fasting and prayer.

ALSO AVAILABLE FROM

JEWISH STORYTELLER PRESS

"Dinezon's writing is poignant and haunting;
his characters are bright, intense, and unforgettable."
—*New York Journal of Books*

"Tina Lunson's excellent English translation (the first ever)
vividly captures mid-nineteenth century Jewish life in
Eastern Europe, revealing not only its particular culture
but also its parallels to today's Jewish experience."
—*Jewish Book Council*

Infusing European literary realism into a Russian-Jewish love
story, Jacob Dinezon's *The Dark Young Man* relates the efforts
of a ruthless husband determined to preserve his authority over
his wife's family by destroying the reputation of her younger sis-
ter's prospective bridegroom. Shady matchmakers and criminal
intrigues conspire to keep the young lovers apart. The novel

evokes themes familiar to readers of Dinezon's more famous colleagues and friends Sholem Aleichem and I. L. Peretz: disparities between rich and poor, the impact of modernity on religious traditions, and the challenges of assimilation on Jewish identity.

Suspenseful and bittersweet, *The Dark Young Man* offers those new to Dinezon's work an excellent introduction. For readers already aware of Dinezon's significance to the Jewish literary canon, the availability of this novel in English provides a meaningful and timely offering.

A tale of suspense, betrayal, love, and death, Dinezon's *The Dark Young Man* is a startling fictional account of mid-nineteenth century Jewish life, culture, and religion by a beloved author and masterful storyteller.

HERSHELE
A JEWISH LOVE STORY

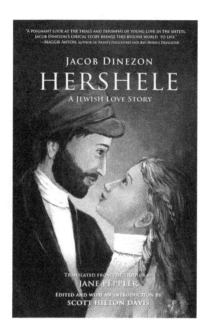

"A gripping tale with a realistic adolescent love story,
a complicated plot, and an unexpected ending."
—*Association of Jewish Libraries Reviews*

"A sweet, ageless romance that has stood the test of time."
—*Foreword Reviews*

In 1891, the Yiddish writer Jacob Dinezon crafted a tender
love story exploring the budding romance between two young
people separated by class and tradition. This compelling fable,
created with equal measures of hope and despair, charmed his
many readers, but until recently, has remained inaccessible to
modern audiences.

Hershele is the bittersweet love story of Hershele and
Mirele—he a penniless yeshiva student with no family, she the

lovely daughter of a widow who provides a weekly charity meal to poor students. Their providential meeting generates an intense attraction that gradually overcomes the powerful obstacles of social norms and class status. But determined forces are arrayed against them, and their first tentative steps towards modernity are challenged at every turn.

Hershele, translated from the Yiddish by Jane Peppler, is at once a fascinating glimpse into the daily life of Eastern European Jews in the late nineteenth century, and the extremely personal and poignant story of two young lovers trapped in the clash between existing traditions and social change. It is simultaneously a historical novel and a timeless tale of romance. In its own way, *Hershele* is the Romeo and Juliet story of the shtetl.

YOSELE

A STORY FROM JEWISH LIFE

"A must-read in this area."
—*Donald J. Weinshank*

In 1899, Jacob Dinezon's short novel, *Yosele,* exposed in vivid detail the outmoded and cruel teaching methods prevalent in the traditional cheders (Jewish elementary schools) of the late 1800s. The novel was so powerful and persuasive, it transformed the Jewish educational system of Eastern Europe.

Writing in Yiddish to reach the broadest Jewish audience, Dinezon described the sad, poverty-stricken, and violent life of a bright and gentle schoolboy whose treatment at the hands of his teacher, parents, and rich society is shocking and painful. The pathos and outrage resulting from the story's initial publication produced an urgent call for reform and set the stage for the establishment of a secular schools movement that transformed Jewish elementary education in the early 1900s.

Translated into English for the first time by Jane Peppler, Jacob Dinezon's *Yosele* presents a dramatic, rarely seen sociological and cultural picture of Eastern European Jewish life at the end of the nineteenth century.

MEMORIES AND SCENES
SHTETL, CHILDHOOD, WRITERS

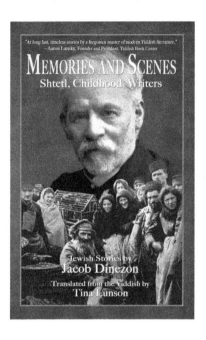

"Jacob Dinezon's newly translated masterpiece belongs next to Sholem Aleichem's works."
—*Forward*

"With Dinezon's *Memories and Scenes,* we happily encounter a master writer who deserves to be ranked with Sholom Aleichem and I. L. Peretz."
—*Hadassah Magazine*

"Highly recommended."
—*Association of Jewish Libraries Reviews*

In August of 2014, the English-speaking world received access to a short-story collection by the once-beloved author Jacob Dinezon, a central figure in the development of Yiddish as a literary language in the second half of the nineteenth century.

Amid poverty and strict adherence to Jewish law and customs, Jacob Dinezon's finely-drawn characters struggle to reconcile heartfelt impulses with age-old religious teachings as modern ideas encroach on their traditional Jewish way of life.

This profound and delightful collection, translated from the Yiddish by Tina Lunson, paints a vivid portrait of late-nineteenth-century Eastern European shtetl life and provides readers with a treasure trove of Jewish history, culture, and values.

JACOB DINEZON
THE MOTHER AMONG OUR CLASSIC YIDDISH WRITERS

"A literary biography with summary, gentle analysis,
and evaluation of Dinezon's works."
—*Jewish Standard*

Was there a fourth classic Yiddish writer? This is what the
renowned literary historian Shmuel Rozshanski asserts in this
insightful and well-documented biography about the beloved
and successful nineteenth-century Yiddish author, Jacob Dinezon (1851-1919), called by the *Forward*, "The Greatest Yiddish
Writer You Never Heard Of."

Credited with writing the first "Jewish Realistic Romance"
and the first bestselling Yiddish novel, Dinezon was closely as-
sociated with the leading Jewish writers of his day, including
Sholem Abramovitsh (Mendele Mocher Sforim), I. L. Peretz,

and Sholem Aleichem—dubbed the "Classic Writers of Modern Yiddish Literature."

Dinezon's poignant stories about Eastern European shtetl and urban life focused on the emotional conflicts affecting Jews of all ages as modern ideas challenged traditional religious practices and social norms. Dinezon was also a staunch advocate of Yiddish as a literary language and a highly respected community activist.

In this extensively researched Yiddish biography written in 1956 and translated into English by Miri Koral, Shmuel Rozshanski makes the case for including Jacob Dinezon in the "family" of classic Yiddish writers. If, as scholars suggest, Sholem Abramovitsh is the grandfather, I. L. Peretz the father, and Sholem Aleichem the grandson of modern Yiddish literature, then Jacob Dinezon, Rozshanski insists, should be considered the "mother" for his gentle, kindhearted, and emotional approach to storytelling and his readers.

An important new research book for scholars of Jewish literature, history, and culture.

To learn more about these
and our other books, please visit

JEWISH STORYTELLER PRESS
www.jewishstorytellerpress.com

CPSIA information can be obtained
at www.ICGtesting.com
Printed in the USA
FSHW011724070321
79264FS

9 780997 533422